PENGUIN · SHORT · FICTION

"Not that the story need be long, but it
will take a long while to make it short."
— Henry David Thoreau

Fables of Brunswick Avenue

Katherine Govier is a native of Edmonton, now living in Toronto with her husband and two children. In 1979 *Random Descent*, her first novel, was published to immediate critical acclaim. Her second novel, *Going Through the Motions*, was published in 1982 and is being adapted for the stage and film. Govier has had stories published in many magazines and has received two national journalism awards. *Fables of Brunswick Avenue* is her first short story collection.

FABLES OF BRUNSWICK AVENUE

Katherine Govier

Penguin Books

Penguin Books Canada Ltd., 2801 John Street, Markham, Ontario, Canada L3R 1B4
Penguin Books Ltd., Harmondsworth, Middlesex, England
Penguin Books, 40 West 23rd Street, New York 10010 U.S.A.
Penguin Books Australia Ltd., Ringwood, Victoria, Australia
Penguin Books (N.Z.) Ltd., Private Bag, Takapuna, Auckland 9, New Zealand

First published by Penguin Books Canada Ltd., 1985

Copyright © Katherine Govier, 1985
All rights reserved.

Manufactured in Canada by Webcom Limited
Typesetting by Jay Tee Graphics Ltd.

Canadian Cataloguing in Publication Data

Govier, Katherine, 1948-
Fables of Brunswick Avenue

(Penguin short fiction)
ISBN 0-14-007578-X.

I. Title. II. Series.

PS8563.085F3 1985 C813'.54 C84-099693-4
PR9199.3.G69F3 1985

Except in the United States of America,
this book is sold subject to the condition
that it shall not, by way of trade or otherwise,
be lent, re-sold, hired out, or otherwise circulated
without the publisher's prior consent in any form
of binding or cover other than that in which it
is published and without a similar condition
including this condition being imposed
on the subsequent purchaser.

Acknowledgements

Some of these stories appeared for the first time, in slightly altered form, in the following magazines:
The Canadian Forum, Descant Magazine, Prism International, Flare, Chatelaine, Cosmopolitan (U.K.), *Honey* (U.K.), *Harper's and Queen.*
Some have appeared in anthologies: "The Dragon," in *Best Canadian Stories, '81*; "The Dancer" in *Stories from Western Canada*; and "The Thief" in *Bakers Dozen.*
"The Thief", "Responding to Pain", "Tongues", and "Going to Europe" have been broadcast on CBC Radio's Anthology.
The author gratefully acknowledges the editors who originally published the stories — Karen Mulhallen, Robert Weaver and others, as well as Cynthia Good of Penguin Books Canada.

For Robin and Emily

Contents

Introduction

Making a book is making something out of nothing, turning an imaginative thing into a marketable thing. Stories are inspirational, but collections are sociological, commodities in fact. They come into being because editors want them to, or because writers discover they finally have enough pages to go between two covers. A fair amount can be told about this book by the story of its cover.

We had decided that we wanted the cover of *Brunswick Avenue* to be a house, or a street of houses. We considered using a photograph, but that seemed too realistic; we thought of having a painting commissioned, but that proved less than realistic for other reasons, namely price. This left as the most likely solution, finding an existing painting to serve.

One name comes up when people speak of painters of Toronto streets: Albert Franck. In Harold Town's book on Franck we found many scenes of the sort we wanted; semi-dilapidated downtown and Annex streets, lanes and backyards. Suddenly he seemed the best artist: he painted one Toronto "bohemia" several decades before I wrote about another, very different one. Some of the houses Franck painted are now gone, in favour of widened streets, new hospitals, subway lines. But those that remain are not much changed — the awkward square back porches and bulging front bays, the half-drawn curtains, above all the colours, that startling brick red on earth and snow. And the place, the geographical spot, is the same — the grid of streets, Spadina, Huron, Gerrard, Robert. We had only to choose the one painting which looked most like Brunswick Avenue.

But what did Brunswick Avenue look like? I went down with a Polaroid; aiming the lens here and there I couldn't get a shot that captured it. I seemed to get cars and glassy renovations or too many wires. But it really didn't matter. As it turned out, the editor had once lived on Brunswick Avenue herself and had her own idea. The art director took a trip by car to see. None of us could actually describe the street, the typical house. It depended on what block you were on, what direction you looked. Surely there was something in the book on Franck. I chose one painting, Spadina Avenue, I think it was, which showed a heavy three-storey house with a large front yard and a tree, beside a wide lane.

"It's lovely, but it doesn't look like Brunswick Avenue. Brunswick Avenue looks like this —" The editor pointed to a painting of a row of narrow gabled Victorians, close to the road and bare. I couldn't agree; it wasn't my Brunswick. We all agreed that a third painting was our favourite, but it was D'Arcy Street.

At this point the art director called the painter's widow.

She asked what the title of the book was to be.

"*Fables of Brunswick Avenue.*"

"But he painted Brunswick Avenue. It's hanging right here, over the mantle."

Excited — now we were going to find the unarguably right painting, the painting to settle all doubts — three of us made our way down to Albert Franck's home in what has become, partly because of his presence there, a neighborhood of galleries, to meet the painter's widow.

I don't know that I stopped to think what I expected in a painter's widow, but if I had, I'd have said an elderly woman surrounded by canvases, respectful, possibly wringing her hands. But the door was opened by a bright, youthful woman who was full of her own ideas. Yes, the house was crammed with paintings, every foot of wall space covered, halls and corners stacked with more canvases and frames, but large numbers of them were hers. The first thing she did was make it clear that she wished to be called Miss Vale.

Our eyes went to the painting over the mantle. There it was, *Brunswick Avenue.* Rather the back yard of a house on Brunswick — large, square, red, snow-stained. It was a lovely painting, but it wasn't — dare I say — it wasn't Brunswick Avenue. It wasn't like what we had begun to think of as our Brunswick Avenue. Maybe it was a bit too much like the real Brunswick Avenue. Still, we were attracted by the idea of literal accuracy. It would be wonderful to be able to say, the cover painting is *Brunswick Avenue*, by Albert Franck. The art director began to assess the picture for its suitability for the format.

Meanwhile Florence Vale was charming us with her artistic output — paintings, new children's stories, a volume of erotic verse — all of which has come since her husband died. "I sit at the breakfast table," I remember her saying, "and it just pours out of me."

Nothing was going as planned. The opinion was that *Brunswick Avenue* wouldn't work. We were not just dealing with a painting, you see, or even with its content. We had to consider the shape of it, whether it was horizontal or vertical, where the things *were* in it, if there was enough sky at the top or if the corner of the house on the right could be cut back without losing the window. I suppose as we spoke about the paintings we sounded a little crass, a little too much like shoppers, a little too critical. It's too this or too that. We meant, too this or that *for our purposes*, but we left that unsaid. We wanted red, we wanted white space at the top for the title, "you see it's part of a series." Miss Vale became just a tiny bit impatient. She defended the way her husband painted things. He was not an illustrator, he was an artist. He had a right to his own Brunswick Avenue.

"You see," said Florence Vale, "he didn't know you were coming."

Sometimes people ask about the different kinds of writing I do. About how a short story collection comes together or about the difference between novels and stories — which is a higher form, and if both aren't higher forms than non-fiction. About the autobiographical content of fiction. An introduction might address some or all of those questions. This one will not. This one is a little fable about what is not.

The cover painting is not Brunswick Avenue, but D'Arcy Street. Florence Vale is not a painter's widow. Short stories or novels are not — or should not be — pre-arranged to suit the literary shoppers. At my best, like Albert Franck, I did not know you were coming.

Although I lived, like the narrator of the first story in this collection, for seven years and at two addresses on Brunswick Avenue; and although I am, like some characters here, a writer, and have, like some other characters, children and unlike some others, a husband; and although the first stories jumped full-blown off the landscape into my lap, they are not like real life. I hope that when they are at their best, they are more like life than life is.

Brunswick Avenue

Brunswick Avenue

Everyone lives on Brunswick Avenue sooner or later. I did more than most, seven years at two addresses, a decade ago. I drove down Brunswick Avenue today and remembered that other September when I first stepped onto the street with my husband. We climbed the stairs of a house with a "Flat for Rent" sign in the window. A compact Chinese woman with an assessing eye came slowly to our knock. And when the transaction was completed, for the third floor rooms were exactly what we wanted, she patted my arm. "I'm Ivy. I like first name best."

I gave her mine; my husband was very shy. We worked back to back in our two rooms. For breaks we used to lie on the bed and discuss whose name would look better on the spine of a book. His was solid and rang true, but was, we agreed, a little easy to forget. We were happy at first, but after a while the place felt small.

Two years later Ivy let me have a larger apartment in

another house. Friends helped me carry the bed, the table, the armchair, and twelve cartons of books across the street and up the stairs; after they finished, I gave them beer and sandwiches. When they left I was frankly, and for the first time in my life, living alone, and I was only beginning to understand what Brunswick Avenue would mean to me.

I still see that second apartment perfectly in my mind. Dark hardwood floors, warped to ridges which I felt with my bare feet as I walked them, claiming the place. Rooms running off a long narrow hallway which I planned to line with books. Facing west, on the front, a sitting room which was cool and dim during the day and briefly glamorized by the low lines of sun towards dusk. And a corner fireplace which actually worked.

That night I rolled my packing paper and burned it in the hearth. When the flames rose, I was ringed by their reflection in the window panes. I threw more and more paper on the flames, feeling the heat, until at last Dawn came pounding on the street door to ask if the house were on fire.

I let the conflagration die and went to the bedroom, where a bay window overhung the paved passageway between my house and the next. I fell asleep to the sound of wooden flutes wafting from a neighbour's window and woke the next morning to voices calling, doors slamming as people went to work. The haphazard division of Victorian houses into flats had created, on this block, a self-addressing world which had the feeling of a camp, struck each night on the same spot, wakened by its inhabitants' need to march — somewhere, anywhere — before resting again. I had come to be alone, but welcomed the borrowed sounds. They were a reminder that my solitary state was chosen, that other lives unrolled close by, that those lives and mine were not unaffected by one another.

From the beginning the Brunswick day fell easily over me, a loose, light garment in which I could hide or be revealed as I wished. As soon as I got up I put on my striped robe and went to the kitchen for coffee. Bearing a blue china cup I went from there to the porch off the back, which had morning sun and a view into the houses all around; that was where I worked at my typewriter. Tapping rapidly from the moment I sat, I could smell, in spring, the arms of the lilac bush scraping on the screen and in winter, vision blurred by plastic stretched over the windows for insulation, hear the drip of melting snow. If I raised my eyes from my work, I could see trees and more windows, alleys, and gardens and enjoy the little neighbourhood mysteries; the man who stored his motorcycle in his house and slept in his garage, the postman who made a regular morning trip up a back fire escape. I could see children smoking cigarettes and kicking heels against the back fences and my friends coming home in the evening with paper bags from the wine store.

"Come and sit on the porch with us!"

"Not now!" I'd wave them away. I wanted to be still and for them to move; I wanted to watch and not be seen. I had the habit of writing by then; I wrote every morning, through lunch. I took the afternoon off and began again after five when kitchen lights went on all around the square and dinners were cooking. I might have kept on until midnight if I hadn't been disturbed. But my friends were persistent. Sometimes they knocked at the door; if I didn't answer they walked right in.

"Come on, you have to eat."

Alarmed, I would jump from the chair and lie across my

papers. My work was present and alive and obvious in that sunporch; it was on my skin; I was as if caught naked with a lover.

"O.K., O.K., let's go," I'd say, slipping the scattered pages into piles, bidding the story presence to fold up with them. And go out to chicken stew in Dawn's basement kitchen or something Hungarian at the Country-Style or just a beer at the Mug. They would have tales of irascible supervisors or humiliating auditions, whatever had happened to them that day. The work might have gone better without these interruptions, but then how would the world have come into it? Much later, with an inward apology to the Brunswick people, I would come back and put a scrap of their conversation in my notes. If they had surprised me in my lair, I caught them too. I was a member of the army encamped on that street, a member like any other, save that I was the one who stopped to write things down.

When my husband and I first chanced onto Brunswick, we were straight out of university in the west and innocent of the ways of these sophisticated urban gypsies. We knew where we wanted to be but not how to get there. Where we wanted to be was in the middle of things, where things happened. Ambition made our love conspiratorial; we alone knew how richly we deserved acknowledgement, not for anything we had done, because we had done nothing, but for everything we might do.

That first year we went upstairs together, shut the door and forgot the outside. We made love and argued, slammed doors, made up, and then made dinner. Our marriage was like a demanding self-obsessed house guest. Invited to parties, we neglected to go down; we said hello to our neighbours without realizing that they wanted to know us. But eventually the guest became a fixture; Hugh and I were released, at least partially, to the world at large.

In my daily, hopeful descents to the front door for mail I had noticed Dawn, stooped, graceful, weighted with long hair, holding conversations on the sidewalk. I had overheard words like "imagery" and "phantom", "inspiration" and "block." She had to be talking about art. One day I spoke to her.

"What do you do?" I said, which was in those days before definitions became firm a permissible question.

She danced. Well, actually she had a bad back and was giving up dancing and would probably study sculpture. In the meantime she was working as an artist's model. Nude, I had to assume. This allowed her the leisure for self-discovery. She said something about exorcising the ghosts of her childhood, during which she had been bedridden. I nodded as if this were the kind of answer offered a stranger every day, when in fact her boldness — not only did she pose without clothes, but she admitted she wanted to be an artist! — stunned me.

"And what do you do?" she asked, laying gentle grey eyes on mine and swaying on her long stem. As she stood, she rubbed her lower back and rolled her shoulders, as if working out a stiffness.

"I write."

"How exciting!" I could tell right away she wanted to know me. That was when my guilt began, for I was convinced that I lied. (I retain this conviction each time I say those words, some twelve years and three books later, which may imply something about me or simply impugn the craft, I don't know.) Back then although I did write I did not publish, and my claim seemed very weak indeed. I covered my confusion, however, by telling her a few things about the story I was working on, being sure I included the words "tone" and "voice" and talked a bit about the difficulties imposed by the first person narrator.

"Do you know Hannah?" said Dawn. Apparently a true, published writer (with a name I recognized) lived on the street. I gushed, but when introductions were offered, I became cautious. Proximity was thrilling, but it was enough for the time being; my imagination leapt ahead to friendship and foresaw problems. I suppose I felt that writers claimed a territory; Hannah's and mine couldn't overlap. I asked more questions. I wanted to know about Hannah, but I was not prepared, not just yet, to know Hannah. When my conversation with Dawn ended, I rushed upstairs and told Hugh all about it. And after I did, I regretted that I had turned my discovery into something else that had to be shared in our cramped space under the sloping ceilings.

It was our second spring on Brunswick when Dawn made a beer stew and we went down to join her party. After that there were many nights on the porch in twilights soft and expansive after the sudden darknesses of winter. Elbows on our knees, bottles beside us, we sat and watched the street and talked more or less as Hugh and I had talked in private.

Our neighbours were like us, striving photographers, potters, film-makers, and graduate students in English or biology; a would-be actress who baked plasticine toys in her oven to sell at subway stops. Livings were put together from part-time teaching, grants, odd jobbing. Everyone was involved in rounds of submissions, auditions, applications; there were never any openings. We had all come from someplace else, and the city seemed to be a conspiracy to keep us out. How extravagantly we complained when a proposal or an exhibition by an unknown was ignored! What fools we thought the critics and custodians of culture! As the summer went on, the porch stoop changed from a place on the sidelines, a repose, to a high vantage point from which an urgent wave of change threatened to break.

Our voices carried across the street until 11 o'clock; then, after we wanted to go in, Hannah would come. Hannah had been, even to my cautious expectations, a disappointment. First, she was old. And then she had practically no conversation, except that which involved herself. She had followed her son, a draft dodger, to Canada; when he had taken amnesty and returned to New York, she was bitter. There was no going back for this veteran of many migrations and marriages. She had a bad heart, a catastrophic cough, and was frequently drunk. Furthermore, she seemed to find us dull.

It occurred to me that I did not understand Hannah. She showed me, once, the contents of her grease-stained knapsack. It had a pocket on either side to make it easier for her to find things. One side, labelled Beauty, had lipstick and scarves for her hair which she combed with her fingers. The other side, labelled Money, was usually empty. In between she kept a supply of self-addressed postcards which she gave away (sometimes with a stamp) to young men she desired, a coil notebook, and, always, a copy of her book, published years before to considerable notice. Hannah wanted people to sing, especially after midnight; unless she found those who were willing, she became hostile and incoherent and had to be led off to bed.

Expeditions to the tavern went and came back. Students pumped their bicycles south to the campus, and panhandlers made their way up from Bloor Street. Young missionaries with slick hair came up from the Church Army

House to ask us to join in their hymns. ''Judgement is approaching,'' they said. ''There is only a little time.'' But we did not want to be saved. Brunswick Avenue was there, moving more and more slowly as summer passed, a carousel in its last few revolutions. The suspense was exquisite; it hurt. I knew something was ending, but I did not know what, until the day Hugh's letter came. He'd been offered a teaching job in the Maritimes; he would take it. I decided to stay behind.

When Hugh left, it was as if a curtain parted; the world saw me and beckoned. Suddenly I knew everyone; after two years I was an old-timer on the street, along with Dawn and a biology student named Redfat. I listened well, and I had a quick way with a phrase; my witticisms were often quoted. The new apartment which Ivy had let me have was the most desirable on the block and added to my stature.

''There are two kinds of people,'' I remember saying. ''There are landladies and then there are the rest of us.'' Ivy was a visible oppressor, walking in her slow, bandy-legged way from one property to another, wandering in and out of our doors without knocking. We joked about her ski pants with tabs under the heels, the maternity smock she wore long after the fact. And what did she think of us? Her habitually lowered brow did not lift when we spoke, although she still insisted on first names.

Perhaps it was this semblance of friendship which first made us angry with Ivy. Her bizarre habits ought to have produced more laughter than rage. She drove an old pink Cadillac with fins, in imitation of some fifties tycoon. The car rolled along Brunswick stopping at angles to the kerb or even on the lawn when she visited a house. I used to find her downstairs in the morning going through our mail. She threw out all official correspondence, regardless of addressee. When once I protested, pulling a letter from the tax department out of the wastebasket, she shook her head.

"You don't want answer those people." A variation of this was "You don't want that man know where you are," which she delivered after sending away any official-looking person who should come looking for me.

"But Ivy, he was a friend."

"I just try help you." Hands went up — there was no accounting for my whims. I was frustrated, but she was enjoying our exchange. But even at her most jolly, the expression of suspicion did not move from her face. She gave nothing away, either avoiding questions or answering in proverbs. When had she come here? Who were the others who lived in her house?

"Ghosts tell no lies," she might say. If I persisted, she'd try to put me off with fake mistakes in English. "What's the matter, you have no sense of human?" was a favourite. The scattered details we discovered only made us wonder more.

The family, so far as we could tell, was extensive. Besides the two small boys, her sons, there was a young man who drove a post office truck and was sometimes "Uncle" sometimes "Brother." There were several sulky teenage girls, sisters or daughters, many "visitors" from China, a silent mother with a face like a walnut, who crept up and down the street carrying small paper bags from the stores. A husband was occasionally mentioned but never appeared. Ivy seemed to be the provider for this complex establishment; indeed, she was its life force. She gardened in several backyards, kept rabbits for stew and chickens for eggs and had two dogs, the smallest of which was said to be trained to kill.

Ivy's domain was no less intimidating: we discovered by

putting our knowledge together that she owned at least ten houses between Dupont and Bloor — numbers 300, 302, 304, and 306 being the ones where we lived. You could always point out Ivy's houses. Their open garages spewed bedsprings and random sinks, the roofs sagged, and the windows were grey with years of dirt. But there was always one redeeming feature — sunflowers by the porch or morning glories climbing the pillars, a certain grace in a turret or archway, something to inspire love.

We laughed, mind you, at the old houses' slow dissolve which seemed designed to thwart their owner. Ivy hated work; as well, she was cheap, careless, and had terrible luck. If, after procrastinating a decade, she finally painted a porch, the next day racoons would eat through the roof over it, and the rain would ruin the job. If she replastered a ceiling, the plumbing on the floor above would leak through it. Ivy's handymen came out of the hotel tavern at the foot of the street; at least once I feared for the life of a pallid rubby on an unstable ladder outside my window. Ivy meanwhile complained of poverty and threatened to sell.

Although she was a millionaire, we were sure, she showed no sign of wealth aside from the Cadillac which usually sat in her driveway, windows open, with children playing in it. She lived in three rooms of such clutter that their purpose — dining, sleeping, sitting — was obscure. The largest was dominated by an iridescent tapestry of a moose glaring over a mountain lake. It was furnished with torn chairs, a card table covered with radio parts and dirty cutlery, and a couple of bicycles. In a doorway an ironing board stood, the perfect Ivy signature, indicating that some effort, albeit beside the point, was being made. It was the same every month when I delivered the rent.

I told my chums about the ironing board and got laughs

for it. It was fun, during nights on the stoop, to speculate on the extent of Ivy's riches and why she lived like we did; or if as she claimed, she weren't rich, who then was the secret slum landlord. It seems to me now a strange obsession. I suppose of all the mysteries before us, she was the one we could lay our fingers on; she was the aspect of this large and callous and thus far unresponsive city within our range. Because we weren't going anywhere, we butted our heads against the place where we had stopped; because she was a sign of our powerlessness, we began to hate her.

Of course without Hugh I had no money. I had to search for work and took it quite for granted when Ivy let my rent go unpaid. She brought me lettuce and beets and carrots from her garden; I hardly noticed. She asked me to go down to Queen Street with her to buy dented tins at a discount. Then she offered one of her dog's puppies to protect my person.

"Women living alone," she said, "got to be careful."

At that point, remembering her own absent husband, I realized that she was making friendly advances; she saw us as being in the same position. I was horrified. I did not want a killer dog; I did not want, in my wildest imagination, to be like Ivy.

I sold a piece of writing. I found a part-time job teaching, and then I sold another piece, this time to a magazine that asked me to do more writing for them. When winter came again, despite the fact that I was still in arrears, I complained of the cold in my apartment. Ivy came to check the radiators. She put her hand on their lukewarm ridges and then turned to me.

"You are too thin. You lose weight since your husband go. He send you money?"

''I'll get money of my own now.''

She grimaced. ''Men not fair to women who have money of their own, don't you think?''

If I thought, I wasn't saying. ''Don't change the subject, Ivy. It's cold in here.'' But she saw the fault as mine. She offered to share a wild deer for the winter; I suppose its meat was to stoke my inner fires. ''We buy one from the Indians, I take half, you take half, then I show you how to cook.''

I gave up, laughing. ''You're too smart for me, Ivy,'' I said and resolved to buy an electric heater, since she paid the hydro bill. We enjoyed our little game.

When finally I had the money to pay my rent, I took it to her door. It was a crisp winter evening and her boys were riding their bicycles under the streetlights. ''Lovely night,'' I said to Ivy. ''So peaceful.'' I felt much more a part of the world, now that I was earning. I suppose I looked triumphant, handing over the cheque.

''You think so?'' She jerked the proffered orange slip of paper in toward her chest; running it between two fingers, she narrowed her eyes. ''I don't think we have peace. I think we have war. Big trucks will push people off the street and there will be dead men everywhere and no food. They even take the bicycles away from those kids.'' She raised her voice. ''Boys! Boys!'' and she made them put their bicycles in the garage and go indoors.

From what past these images came I was never to know. I don't think I cared where she learned to see conspiracies and disaster in a quiet city street full of gentle people, few of whom were hungry. But the lights came on as we stood there; suddenly I wanted to thank her for the Brunswick world that was a haven to me. I muttered a few words about liking my apartment, and then I was off.

My friendship with Ivy was becoming awkward. She disliked my knowing the others, as if she feared we would gang up against her. Her response to our nightly gatherings was to tell me tales about my fellows. This one stole furniture and that one pulled down light fixtures. Redfat was a bad man and very dirty; Hannah ought to be in a mental hospital. There were particles of truth in all of what she said, but Ivy knew me not at all if she thought I would abandon my friends for mere irresponsibility or vice.

Brunswick was at its height then. Looking back, I see mine as a nearly perfect life. I wonder how many of us have found its better? Sunlight fell through my back window in the morning and toward evening skimmed over the rooftops to enter the porch over the street. When good news came for me in the mail, there were three or four friends nearby to dance on the lawn in celebration. We were in and out of each other's apartments for teabags and money and records. We loved our tacky camp and all our possibilities. The street belonged to us for the time we were there. Years could go by without my wanting to leave, and years did.

The beginning of the end came with another summer — my fifth — and cockroaches. One day Redfat came out of his basement to say that he'd noticed some bugs in his oven. I went down into his dark kitchen and turned on the light. There was a general scuttle so fast I blinked; something dark on the walls, like a fine net, had dissolved in an instant. I looked closer. The things were everywhere, down behind the sink and taps, along the cracks of the kitchen counter, even in the rubber stripping along the fridge door.

"How can you stand it in here?" I asked.

"I never noticed," he said, shifting his feet. Chanting

his mantra or sorting his dried weeds, he was oblivious to such detail.

"But Red —" I wailed. I didn't bother to explain what I knew. Because I lived above him and the other houses were attached, it would soon be evident he had roaches; we would all have roaches. In a week I found their traces, the black dust on shelves, transparent egg-cases in corners from which barely visible miniature versions crawled out to instant maturity. One day I reached in my kitchen cupboard for my blue cup and put my finger on a roach resting on the handle. I screamed and threw the cup across the room, smashing it.

Before that day in Redfat's kitchen, roaches had lived for me only in fable. I had heard they grew to the size of thumbs in Houston, and accepted that in certain New York hotels a few lazy black specimens could be seen by tourists. But these before me were small and brown and fast and successful beyond imagination. At first I attacked their numbers with spray insecticide. They increased. I tried boric acid. They thrived. My kitchen, with its crooked walls, old gas stove, and warped floorboards which were impossible to clean, was ideal for them.

Infestation gave my apartment a new and sinister identity. My quaint abode had gone over to another side of life. I had come from a cosmetic suburb where any show of human habitation from a neighbour was an affront; garbage cans, naked children, voices raised in anger, all like unpleasantness was carefully hidden. That was why Brunswick's gypsy-camp openness had charmed me so. But the vision of Red's kitchen stayed with me. I knew instantly that it was one thing to live in an eighty-year-old, patched and partitioned house among colourful eccentrics, and it was quite another to have bugs.

As it happened, the others were much like me. Roaches made our chic flats squalid; from this point urban poverty yawned before us, and we were on our way up, not down. Something had to be done. It took only days to discover that individual action was futile. Four of us went together to Ivy's door to demand she fumigate.

Demand, I say, and give away our mistake. Ivy stood half behind her door, her eyes hooking mine, her face more stubborn and blank with each word we spoke. To give in to a demand would have been beneath her dignity. If getting rid of the cockroaches had been our only aim, announcing helplessness and speaking ill of Red would have served us better. Perhaps because of my "friendship" with Ivy, I, more than the others, did understand, but I was too angry to take the easy way.

"Get rid of them," I said. "You have to."

She laughed. "Cockroaches very old. They been living one million years."

"Not in our houses," we said.

She shrugged. "They don't bite."

Assuring us that a little poisoned sugar along the baseboards (Poisoned sugar! What about my cats!) would do the trick, she closed the door in our faces.

Across the street, we gathered. Others were notified as they came home from work; the cockroach crisis would require a meeting of tenants. My apartment being the largest, I became the host. We would have none of Ivy's fatalism; there would be no giving up in the face of this threat to our homes. Human beings could not live in these conditions. There were laws about such things. We agreed to act; knowing all about Ivy's delays and half-hearted efforts, we would circumvent her and call in the authorities. And while we had their attention, we could ask for a few improvements in the houses — the water pressure was bad, we really needed some door bells, and none of our refrigerator freezing compartments was cold enough.

Dawn raised a point. She had given up sculpture by then and was following the Maharaji Ji; she was full of love for the world. ''Ivy gives me lettuce,'' she said. ''She doesn't raise the rent; she's my friend.''

''Can you live off her lettuce? Are you a rabbit? Even her rabbits end up in the stew. If she cared about you, do you think she'd expect you to put up with all this?'' I was persuasive, and Dawn was overruled.

I placed the first call myself the next morning. I'd been doing some writing for a newspaper and had learned how to deal with the city. I used a punchy phrase here, a suggested threat there, and all around a firm, determined voice. Within a week health inspectors had come and fumigation was ordered. After several sprayings the cockroaches were beaten; they died or moved on down the street. But there was more to come — inspectors from other city departments. Fire prevention, building, and zoning standards had to be met. There was a great flurry of action by the end of which Ivy was presented with a list of one hundred and eight improvements to make.

Well! That was action. We tenants had copies of this list. My apartment appeared as ''Second floor south. Front room, inadequate ventilation. Bathroom unsafe, tiles cracked. Back porch uninhabitable, ceiling too low. . .'' We celebrated our victory, but I had a cold feeling; it was as if a loved one in perfect health had been taken in for examination and was assessed as having little chance of survival.

Ivy was given ninety days to make these repairs. Nothing happened during that time; that was no surprise. Next a more insistent demand, in the form of a poster with black lettering, was posted on the door of each faulty house. After one hundred and twenty days the houses would be deemed unfit for human habitation and would be closed. Face to face with this edict, we were given pause. "Will we have to move?" I said to the inspector, who was confidently pocketing his thumbtacks. He reassured me: these threats were always effective. I wanted to believe that, and indeed Ivy appeared to have capitulated. Estimators began to appear, examining chimneys and stairways and windows and then going away leaving all as before.

The poster curled and turned brown and fell off the door. Ivy disappeared. There were rumours that she was in China, in Florida, even in jail. One hundred and twenty days passed; the inspector came around, but he couldn't do anything, he said, until he could find Ivy. For one whole winter the pink Cadillac did not move, and rent was collected by sister/daughters or uncle/brothers.

It was a sullen spring day, as cold and damp as April can be in Toronto, when I walked up from Bloor to see a suntanned Ivy standing in her driveway. She hailed me, as she would have in old times. She didn't want to talk about Florida. Around her feet were cardboard cartons; she opened one to show me bags and bags of French-fried potatoes.

"They given away free," she said, "to non-profit organizations."

I could see the McCann's truck parked in front of the Church Army House and guessed that there had been a warehouse fire somewhere and that Ivy, along with the missionaries, was reaping the benefit. She was very pleased with her new phrase.

"Take some," she said, "I give them to you. I'm non-profit." She smiled wickedly. I couldn't ignore the challenge.

"Come on, Ivy, you went south for the winter while we sat here freezing in your apartments. You're rich."

"No," she said. "Not me. You people, you rich. Not me. Wait and see," she said, pressing half a dozen bags of potatoes into my arms, giving me her contradictory, sly grin. "Share them," she said. "Give some to Dawn." I went off with my arms full.

Perhaps Ivy thought that was the end of it: she could put down the revolt with evasion, climaxed by a bit of theatre. And she might well have been right. Some complicated legal procedure was said to be underway at City Hall, but we had lost interest. Tired of our campaign and perhaps a little ashamed, we were almost content to stop there. And why did we not? Partly because the grievance, though displaced, was real and partly because we couldn't: the dragging, seemingly ineffectual oxen of government were pulling, even though they could not be seen. The solution was to make a gesture: we took a collection and hired a lawyer. This man was eloquent on the subject of our rights, and he did something simple and wonderful. He asked us what we wanted. He asked each of us to lay out in detail the improvements we sought for our quarters. Then he took these demands away and had them typed.

So it was, one day I stood on the porch reading a new version of Brunswick Avenue, neat on bond with stapled pages. It was noon, and spring. The archway of branches over the street was still transparent, lightly touched with lemon-yellow buds. Sun made the gables and porches as sharp as pencil lines against the cardboard blue sky. Every brick on every house stood out in definition: I could have counted them. When I finished, I threw back my head and laughed aloud. It wasn't funny, it was just that I finally understood.

There was nothing wrong with Brunswick Avenue except that we had lived there too long, and for too long no one had asked us what we wanted. What we wanted: in other terms, the contents of Hannah's bag, Beauty and Money and Fame. But while those eluded us, here in such close quarters with others who strove, we would settle for new doorbells, freezer doors, plaster, and carpets; hotter water, fire escapes, and mailboxes. Snow shovelling in winter, outdoor lights in the parking lot, an intercom system, and a paint job. It had seemed reasonable enough, bit by bit. But pressed into type, under letterhead, I could see that it was not Brunswick Avenue at all, but a draft for another world.

In certain lights, I now have beauty and money and fame. I have published books (my ex-husband has published more) and I live in a house of my own. Occasionally I am invited to read from my works. A small number of people recognize my face from television. When I gave my notice on Brunswick it was nothing to apologize for. It was simply time to move on; I thought I might get married, I might even have children.

I wasn't the first to leave. Dawn had found our struggle too mundane and had gone to live with other converts to her religion. Redfat was evicted, Ivy's single scapegoat. His basement was rented to two members of a motorcycle group. With my house half empty, I was frightened. I heard noises above me in the night, and when I asked Ivy who was living there, she looked at me slyly. "Ghosts living there," she said.

That was why on moving day none of the old people were there to help me go; my new man waited out in front in his truck as I gave the key to the lesbian caterer who was taking over the fabulous apartment. I might have driven away without saying goodbye except that Ivy came down her driveway. I realized she'd been watching us load. Was she checking to see that I didn't take the light fixtures or throw paint on the floor? Perhaps. She saluted. I could not interpret the signal.

"You been living here long time," she said. "I will miss you."

Today as I drove down Brunswick I noticed our houses, numbers 300, 302, 304, and 306, had been renovated and were for sale. Could it be that at last the legions of witless inspectors had their way? Then I passed a tall, graceful woman leaning over a child on a bicycle, and her posture called back years before. The slight curve in the spine, the hair still long but now streaked brown and loosely tied. It was Dawn. Recognizing her gave me a shock, as if I had unexpectedly run into a forgotten member of my family.

It had happened before: after I moved I had bumped into her on Avenue Road. She had renamed herself Halley after the comet and was wearing a sari. "I tried art," she had said then, "but it was too hard. I tried political action (she meant our tenants' union) but there was no love in it. Now He is giving me everything." I was angry then; today I realized that I always thought her silly.

I stopped, and she introduced me to her son. I asked Dawn what she was doing — the question that made us friends, that eventually set her to such pirouettes of self-examination and excuse, and that ultimately divided us.

"Nothing," she said carelessly and began to rub the boy's back as if he were a baby and needed to burp. The boy was ill, she said; she had just spent three weeks sleeping beside his hospital bed. I was unprepared and said something banal like perhaps he'll grow out of it. Her eyes, which always glowed, grew brighter with tears; perhaps not. We spoke a little longer, but he was whining and wanted to go home. I was out of my depth; I didn't know how to discuss this tragedy. Perhaps I was feeling a little outdone by my old friend.

"Do you live here again?" I said. I had been lonely over the years and had considered moving back myself, but it would have seemed like slipping.

"Oh no, I just come down to see Hannah," she said. "She's getting her old age money now. She hasn't got a thing, but she makes it look good. Like these pigeons she's a scavenger, but she does all right. Ivy won't take any rent."

"She still owns houses here then?"

"A few," said Dawn. I imagined her eyes to be full of accusations, and perhaps they were.

"The old life," I said lightly. "It was good at the time, but you'll not see me there again, not if I can help it."

Dawn said nothing. I stared at her and wondered if in her child she had found the perfect occupation, the one without compromise. "You're very brave," I said, or should have said.

She touched her hair. "I had no choice." And then, as she turned to go, "You've done well."

Did I imagine the distaste in her voice? Why did I not tell her I had no choice either? Of course, it wasn't true; I was very deliberate in my becoming. It was just that I wanted Brunswick Avenue to forgive me; I believed I was faithful to it. Apologies were definitely not in order, for after all I had done what the rest of us only talked about. But still she seemed superior; she made me feel unclean. Dawn had become content, and I was still greedy for more.

And that was not the worst of it, I realized as I faced her, all possible words draining from my throat. I thought of all we had said in our inexperience, our arrogance, about how beauty was bestowed by admiration, and money and fame got by compromise. She knew only too well what I had done; we had been that clever in our imaginings. If I had risen it was by using them; one of me required many of them in the background, living lives of pain and joy somehow more meaningful than my own. The battle with Ivy had been only a surface. The real battle was among us; it was the struggle to break out of the group, to have the power. If alliances were to be drawn now, it would be Dawn and Hannah and even Ivy against me. I was the other, the leech, the landlady. That was what she saw, and I saw her seeing it, and I had no way to contradict her.

I said goodbye to Dawn. I will run into her again on a street because that's the way this city is, but our long conversation over the years has closed. What she was, what they all were to me is over and done with. I have the stories, of course, but that is only half of it.

The Thief

The Thief

She wasn't just any woman. For that reason she saw no others of her sex as threats to her safe place in her husband's affections. But one night while she slept in their bed, high in one of those columns that push up from the city into the quilt of night, a fault opened up in her world.

She woke, instantly alert. She touched the space beside her. Her husband was not there. The knowledge that he was with another woman had wakened her; sleep dissolved.

She sat until dawn, her long black hair around her neck like a cowl, the heel of her hand pressed into her mouth to stop herself from crying. When her husband arrived, she was composed. He confessed to being with another woman and even to loving this other, a young girl of their acquaintance. The wife smiled to know she'd been right. She urged that he go to his new love. She displayed no passion, choosing to keep her pride intact. She packed a bag and left, pressing the side of his head against hers. They'd never be together again.

She found a small attic apartment in an old house on Brunswick Avenue, one of those shabby streets shadowed by downtown highrises. The walls were stained from the traffic of other lives, a splotch of wine here, a gouge from a nail there. She puttied up the holes and painted it all relentless white. Adding objects like letters to a page, she made it her own. Indian print fabric to drape over the old couch, a wicker chest that had belonged to her mother, a crouching armchair bought from the junk dealer, and a Japanese table at which she could sit cross-legged to eat. She hung a map of the world and a mirror on the wall. It was all hers; nothing admitted the existence of another person. She sat and said her name over to herself. Margaret.

The attic bedroom had low walls that converged over the centre of the room. The threaded reflection of daylight passed into the room narrowly through a window that looked into the next roof. Margaret hung her clothes in the closet and placed her hairbrush on the dresser and sat out her nights by herself. She was not unhappy; she felt safe.

Often she lay on her new bed, which had an old iron frame painted white, and looked through the uncurtained window, letting her eyes sink into the darkness. Or she stared at the point where the slanted walls met in the ceiling. She dozed and culled images from her dreams, like someone feeding herself after a long fast. She lay on her side sometimes, curled like a snail, and thought about the woman she had become, lonely, and having to invent her life again.

It was a minimal sort of life. She carried on with her job teaching small children and was more than normally tender with them. She was so restrained with her associates that they almost began to fear her. When she wanted to see people again she called up other single women to go to movies. She was invited out to dinner by couples who nervously vowed to be friends with her and her ex-husband, about whom they offered news without referring to his young woman. But at their dinner parties, alone among marrieds or paired with some strange bachelor, she felt a worm of bitterness start in the pit of her stomach. She brazened it out by not believing herself pathetic. But more and more, as the world held up its mirrors, she began to see herself as a victim of a crime.

Until then Margaret had viewed the girl, who was pale with a moon face and a high round forehead like a madonna's, as much lesser than herself. The loss had therefore not been a defeat but a sad manifestation of the weakness of her husband, that was all. But now the moon face, white and unshadowed, rose up in her dreams like a rival. Thinking of the girl, she cried as she had never cried before.

She had been avoiding men. Even at a stand-up gathering, Margaret found herself automatically steering away from men who attracted her. It was because when faced with a man, she could speak nothing but lies. She had to flatter him, but she looked at his face and saw a poor creature who would be fooled this way. But her friends taught her she was lonely, that she needed a man, that she needed, even, to avenge herself after being cast off. A decent interval passed, and people began to offer Margaret introductions. But she was numb to the heart and out of practice; sex and love, she thought, were the sport of those more nimble than she. Months of undisturbed sleep in her own bed had made her a virgin again. She had several overt offers from men she met in bars, at parties, men who sought out women like her. She declined them. She met a teacher who interested her, but that night she dreamed he broke into her room and the next day she couldn't speak to him. It was three seasons since she'd left her husband before Margaret found herself actually looking for a man.

The first one was an unlikely choice. He lived on her street, and sometimes as Margaret walked in or out she saw him drive by, his rusty-bottomed Chevrolet chugging softly, his hands poised gently at the top of the steering wheel. One day she was waiting at the cash in the corner store when he appeared behind her, holding a jug of milk. He was tall and very thin, with longish hair, and a profile that could have been drawn from an Egyptian tomb. He said his name was James. He offered her a ride home. She asked him in, and he sat awkwardly on the couch. When he commented on the stein in which she served his beer, she explained that it was booty from her wedding. James was delighted to hear she was divorced; his wife had left him only two months before. They grew animated, exchanging sad stories until it was time for James to leave.

In a few days he called her, and they agreed to go to a movie. James drove a little too fast that night; she sat hard against the door. The film had a lot of sex in it. When the hero laid his hand on the heroine's breast, a grainy dune slung across the thirty-foot screen, Margaret was embarrassed. When the movie star bodies began to heave like worlds in birth under the lights, James shifted his narrow hips away from her on the sprung seats. Leaving, they held hands in commiseration. They went to a bar and he drank three beers, sliding lower and lower in his chair. She leaned over her vermouth and nibbled a swizzle stick.

Romantic love had dropped between them like a stage façade, tacky, overdrawn, and irresistible. They both knew what had to come. He had drunk a little too much; in the car he pulled her beside him and dropped his lank arm over her shoulder. At the house, she asked him in.

They said nothing as they climbed the flights of stairs to her attic. James's feet thudded loosely behind Margaret, as if his shoes were too big. He wanted neither tea nor coffee, but shored himself in the corner of her couch, muttering about his wife. She moved nervously from wall to window, finding nowhere to sit. When she came near, he flung his arm around her and pulled her down beside him. They stayed like that for a while, looking at the opposite wall, their breath coming separate and fast.

When his arm grew tight on her shoulder, she went limp. He pulled her around in front of him and kissed her hard, pressing her lips back into her teeth and then forcing them apart with his tongue, which was as rough as a horse's. She noted he was disturbing the printed cover on her couch. But he seemed to know what he was doing, and she relinquished herself.

His breathing went deeper into his abdomen. He thrust her sideways suddenly to get himself horizontal and pulled her down beside him. He kicked off his loose shoes, which clomped to the floor. Then he rolled down onto her. She was acutely conscious of her backbone pressing into the seam of the couch and of her neck jammed against the arm of it. To relieve the pressure, she strove for greater limpness. He ground his hard genitals into the side of her hip. Fearing for her neck and quite unable to breathe, she tried to find her hands and press her head upward.

"Why don't we go to the bedroom?" she asked.

The tension suddenly went out of James. Looking quizzical, he hoisted his weight off her. He pushed his hair back into place and sat up, stabbing around on the floor for his shoes like a blind man. Margaret sat up and felt her neck cautiously. It seemed to be intact. She was so grateful to be able to breathe that she touched his hand tenderly. James found his shoes and picked them up, heels together, in one hand. They stood and walked to the bedroom. He placed his shoes neatly outside the door.

They lay down beside each other on their backs, acquiescent before the imperative. They were still, still, still. Margaret wanted to encourage James, lying meek and mournful as he was, but she saw now that she had erred. In taking the lead, she had disarmed him. She stared straight up to the point where the walls met over her and thought about the night sky beyond her ceiling. She touched James's belt buckle; he flipped over and lay flat on top of her.

Not speaking, keeping their faces firmly tucked by the chin over each other's shoulders, they moved about exploratively, two opposite contours searching for a fit. James undid the buttons of her blouse and drew it off her, carefully, and then dropped it over the edge of the bed. She undid the buttons of his shirt, and he shrugged himself out of it. She took off her tights and her skirt, while he rattled his buckle and curled himself out of his pants. Modest in their briefs, they pulled up the bedspread and slid themselves under it.

A kind of vacancy settled on them then. The awful truth was that neither of them wanted to make love now, and it was too late to retreat. The only way was forward, to get the thing done. Margaret retrieved her hand from under his side and slid it into his shorts. It was warm in there and incredibly soft. She felt she was invading some poor animal's nest. There was no movement. She let her hand stay there, feeling in the tangle of hair. Still nothing. She panicked and withdrew. She felt hopelessly undesirable. She wanted to rid herself of this man, this terrible mistake in her bed.

He lay there. Margaret yawned ostentatiously. She could hardly bear to hear his excuses when they began to come out — that he'd drunk too much, that he didn't know her well enough. How well had he known her when he pinioned her on the couch? She made light of it. She apologized. She would have done anything to make him leave, but he made no move. He seemed about to fall asleep.

"Are you going home?" she said. She especially wanted his shoes removed from where she could see them, just outside the bedroom door. "Please," she said, "I wish you'd go." It was difficult to be firm, but she just couldn't bear him to be there. "I won't be able to sleep if you stay," she said.

But he was not going to go. He roused himself to become adamant. He'd claim the territory one way or another; leaving then would have been the final defeat. In consideration of his assaulted manhood, Margaret did not make a scene. She rolled away, taking her hips as far as possible from the heat sent off by his lank body, and pretended to sleep. She was angry all night and afraid to move for fear he'd know she was awake.

At dawn he approached her again, and again was impotent. At eight o'clock she got up to go, put on her robe, and went out to make coffee. He slept until she was standing by the bed, fully dressed, holding his clothes. She turned her back to him and let him slide out of the bed. She could hardly speak for hating him. He kissed her proprietorially and patted her hips before scuffing down the stairs and out the door.

It took her days to get over shuddering when she thought of that night. James called again, with a kind of leer in his voice, suggesting there was some rite in their history to be reenacted. She was rude in refusing.

Weeks later, at a party, Margaret met a short, thick-haired man with hawkish eyes. She circled the room talking to this one and that, but he watched her continuously. He asked if he could telephone. She gave a quizzical incline of her head and left the party, nearly forgetting him. But he did call, saying his name again, which was Raoul. He courted her with such tact and insistence it was a whole month before she realized what he wanted.

He wanted her. He was wise; he would let her get used to the idea; he was careful not to overwhelm her. Sometimes he leaned toward her across a table with a look so intense she had to turn away to avoid being consumed. But most often he held himself back. She really only let him come around because she felt she could be immune to him.

But one night, at the beginning of a holiday weekend, they sat in Margaret's apartment with a bottle of wine nearly empty between them. The telephone rang. It was her ex-husband, calling to see how she was getting along. She could hear the young woman like a soprano part in his voice. She wished she could connect again, be intimate as she had been with him. She looked over at Raoul as she spoke and felt something cracking — pity? vengeance? love? When she replaced the receiver, she took Raoul's hand between her palms and pressed it. There was a pulse inside.

They left her apartment with arms slipped across each other's backs, went to his place, and built a fire. He had been waiting for this for a long time. His house was lined like the gentlest of traps. He slid cushions under her head and back as he eased her down to the rug. He explored her with stubby fingers which sensed her skin like some sea plant. He murmured things like, "Now just raise your arm," and, "We'll have you out of this in one minute," as he undressed her.

Raoul bare-chested, Margaret wrapped in a throw rug and clutching most of her clothes, they moved to the bedroom. He flicked a switch; the light dimmed and a melody strained from the corners. He was so delicate and dedicated that their bodies were drawn up together, sounding one long, mellow chord. Afterwards she did not even want to turn her face away, he was so comforting.

And then the room was dark. She slept, or else didn't know waking from sleep. His breathing was soft and insensate. She could see and hear nothing else at all; the dark seemed to come from inside of him. The night had nearly passed when she felt him move and then there was again the progress of those weaving antennae over her skin.

He told her he loved her. He wanted to be with her all the time. He was even hurt when she looked out the window during breakfast. He laughed when she joked, and his anger was roused by her troubles. They told each other stories to make a past for themselves, but she found herself less interested in him than in herself-through-him. He was joyful, and she was generous, like a hostess at her own body, pleased to see him enjoying himself.

At the end of the weekend she went home. Her white apartment had borne her absence like a cheated spouse; the refrigerator was sour, the plants drooping. She cleaned and dusted and sat alone with the radio on the chair opposite. She slept in her own bed again. Then Raoul called, and the affair began in earnest.

At her place, he sulked. He found the chairs uncomfortable, the walls glaring, the sink too low. The next night she went to his place and found herself going there regularly, as to a recurring dream. He cooked her omelettes for breakfast and kissed her goodbye on the street corner; when he repeated "I love you" the words hung overhead like an accusation.

Something was wrong. At night she lay in the dark of his room trying to make out the lines of furniture, the black glint of a mirror. She fought to hide her sleeplessness, but he could feel it. His voice came to her from sleep. "You're awake, Margaret," he said. "Sleep." Like a hypnotist. "Sleep." Instead she made love to him, then wanted to go home. Raoul offered to walk with her, but she wouldn't let him. He lay on his back, his eyes like the coals of a fire kicked apart to burn itself out. She walked slowly under the streetlights. In her own bed again she slept heavily, pushing back dreams of the madonna-faced young woman.

She decided that the problem had been that Raoul loved her too much: his need made a circle within which she could not exist. She thought herself wicked for this; she had been suspicious, like an animal in a strange den, fearing ambush. Now Margaret was doubly alone, having been not only the abandoned one but the abandoner. She repotted her plants and washed the windows. She thought of her husband as she worked and of how rare their love had been. The image of the girl who had stolen him from her made her want to kill, to kill the thief, but more, to kill the new outlaw in herself.

Because all the men she met now seemed to be married, Margaret knew about this problem; she'd heard other women refer to it, but she'd never seen herself as one of those other women, those predators. She would walk into a bar and sit at a counter. On her right would be a man in a pin-striped suit; he would turn to smile at her. Even without a wedding ring on his finger he looked married. Behind his eyes would be a woman, patiently waiting in the passenger's seat of a wide, chrome-toothed car or laying out the trousseau flatware on a teak table, not looking at the clock, refusing to know how late her husband was, or where in the cold sprawl of the city he was sitting, smiling down a bar counter. She would pay for her drink and leave.

But.

Sam was a married man. He walked into her classroom to inspect her teaching and stood at the back, one knee bent, hands in his belt loops, smoking where smoking was not allowed. They had lunch. He reached to look at a ring on her right hand. When he touched her, she jerked the hand back, but he'd caught it firmly. His eyes seemed to say, "I can do this if I want." They talked, but it was like walking a wet slope, the ground disappearing under them. Margaret kept slipping, losing words, losing focus, sliding toward him.

It was only lunches at first, and then it was dinners. One day he arrived with a gift, and she knew he'd decided to make her his lover. She was flattered. Sam would take her to dinner, and then they'd go back to Margaret's place, drink brandy on the couch, and at 10 o'clock they'd go to bed. At midnight he would get up to go home. It happened many times, just that way. She lay with the sheets tucked over her breasts and watched him dress for his wife, untidily, tie and collar undone, as if he wished his treachery to be discovered.

Margaret told herself that the wife did not matter, that if Sam had affairs it meant there was something wrong with his marriage, so that if it weren't her, it would be someone else. She told herself she was not guilty, she was only a witness. Until, fatally, Margaret developed her own possessiveness and grew curious about Sam's wife. Before midnight, sitting up in bed smoking a cigarette, Sam talked about her. She was a tall redhead and liked walking a lot; she would sometimes walk alone for hours just for the pleasure of moving. He puffed on his cigarette contemplatively and said he would be leaving her soon. Margaret sat absolutely still and looked at the starlight coming in the narrow window. She could see the wife come in the door downstairs and start toward her, sometimes with her children following.

At first this image gave Margaret a certain pleasure. She felt included in the family as Sam spoke; it was so easy to be the other woman. Certainly she fancied some day it would end, that Sam would indeed leave his wife and they would be together, but she let this future rest somewhere rather distant. Sometimes before midnight she even looked at the clock.

One night it all changed.

"I thought I wouldn't go," said Sam.

Margaret exclaimed in gratitude and hugged him. But in the cages of her bones something began to move, something terrible and familiar. The image of the wife gathered power, threatened the landing of her safe apartment. She wished she knew nothing about this woman who walked just for the pleasure of walking.

They had dinner and an extra brandy each. They went to wash, brushed shoulders in the narrow hallway, and said "excuse me" like travellers in a hotel. They went to bed and made love. A coiling and uncoiling animal beside Margaret counteracted the movements of their bodies. They finished, and Sam went off to sleep, a child holding his stuffed animal. She loosened his arms from around her body and sat up.

She saw the red-headed wife walking across the floor,

and above her the ceiling flew off. The sky was blue-black with brilliant stars pricking out like tiny holes to some brighter place. Then she saw the wife in her bed, waking, and screaming, and forcing the heel of her hand to her mouth to stop herself. She felt the pain lash at the red-headed wife and at her own heart, and she knew she'd met herself again. Now she saw the moon-faced girl sleeping beside her own husband. She reached out into the image to waken the girl, to warn her, so that she too would sit up beside the sleeping man and cry out before it was too late. Because it was really the three of them, the madonna girl, the wife, and Margaret who belonged to each other and must speak. She wanted to reach out both arms to seize the hands of the two other women, to hold hands, and make a circle. But she sat, legs shrouded in sheets, and made no move.

Responding to Pain

Responding to Pain

"You should have got an ambulance for this, lady." The taxi-driver was a whiner, and he didn't know the one-way streets so it took them forever to get to the hospital. Sara sat beside Jackie in the back seat, propping her up with an arm around her small shoulder. The unconscious woman couldn't weigh more than one hundred pounds, still, Sara had had to get one of the stoned film-makers to help carry her friend out of the house.

At the hospital she answered the questions. Age, twenty-six; occupation, proof-reader. Jackie would have felt poorly represented by her job title. Sara added a slash and "poet." She produced Jackie's medical insurance (expired) from the purse she'd picked up in her room. No evidence of foul play, history of drug abuse extensive. Details unknown. Sara went to the waiting room and sat for two hours watching the clock. Finally a doctor came out.

"Are you her next of kin?"

"Her parents live in Halifax."

"They should be notified. And it would help if you could find out what she took. She's still deeply comatose. She's not responding to anything."

It was after one o'clock in the morning. The night before Sara had begun calling Jackie at seven. The telephone rang and rang: Sara could picture the small, neat room where it sat. The noise would seem like a violence in the silence. Jackie had not turned up for their regular jogging at six. That was not surprising, but they'd had a date for dinner after. The dinner date wasn't something you'd just forget about, not for Sara. When there was no answer by eight o'clock, Sara had gone down to the fish and chip place and had eaten slowly, thinking over the things she'd been planning to tell Jackie that night. The number of phone calls she'd had at the office this morning over the show on Saturday and the tension in her back from crooking her neck around the receiver. The way the producer had looked at her in story meetings when she had made a suggestion: God, you'd have thought she was speaking Russian. By nine o'clock she was home again, and Jackie still did not answer her telephone.

Sara listened to the ringing and tried to think. When had she last seen Jackie? Noon on Sunday was the last time she'd spoken to her, and that was over the telephone. She hated the telephone, impotent snaky black thing in her hand, a pretence at communication. Who would know where Jackie had been for a day and a half? She called Jackie's landlady. The landlady was having a party to celebrate the completion of her company's first film.

"I haven't seen her all day," she shouted. "But the

light's been on in her room since last night. I've heard the phone ringing so I assume she spent the night out somewhere."

The night out. Sara put down the receiver. With the man she talked about. Sara's heart began to pound. She started calling around — people who might have seen her or who knew who this man was. Joanne wasn't home. Don wasn't home. Don's boss wasn't home. Ellen had her answering service on. Someone knew the man's name but not his number. Twenty calls later, Sara threw the telephone against the wall. It began to beep. At eleven o'clock she left her house in a taxi and went to Jackie's place. She had decided to look in her room to see what coat she'd been wearing and then go to the police.

Outside the brick front she asked the driver to wait. She opened the front door without knocking, knowing it would be unlocked as always.

The landlady's guests stood in curls of smoke staring past one another's shoulders. She heard an Elvis Costello record and talk about rushes. Taking the stairs, Sara turned her back on the party. She was nervous: her breath was short as she climbed to the second floor where Jackie stayed, a second class member of a non-family. Suddenly the landlady was there, darting past her, apologizing, and saying she should have checked the room herself. Duty struggling to replace drink on her face, the landlady ran across the second floor landing ahead of Sara and opened the door to Jackie's room.

Autumn had come to the room that day. All the small prizes of Jackie's world — the flowered shawls, old buttons, curling postcards — the minute, sentimental trinkets she captured in junk stores along Queen Street and placed in faultless formation on the walls and ledges had been knocked to the floor. Jackie was hardly visible where she lay on the bed, crumpled in the midst of her coats and dresses, her feet curled under her and her head dropping sideways. She looked like a newspaper blown against a fence.

"Oh, look, she's only sleeping." The landlady's face relaxed into an idiotic grin.

Sara stepped in front of her and reached for her friend.

A long straw of spittle was hanging from Jackie's mouth and had made a pool on the spread. Her head rolled when Sara tried to sit her up. Her eyes, when Sara lifted the lids, were star blue and black, the seeing part vacant as space. The irrelevance of eyes without consciousness impressed her. Sara's relief, the smile that had started up on her face at the sight of Jackie, was fading. But she wasn't afraid yet: Jackie's body was warm, very warm, and she was breathing. The warmth was what she clung to.

After listening to the doctor, Sara took another cab back to the house where Jackie rented her room. The party was quieter now. Several guests had settled in for the night in the living room. Sifting through the detritus in her friend's room, Sara found an empty bottle of prescription pills. She called Jackie's parents and then a cab to go back to the hospital with the bottle. She gave it to the doctor, but he did not seem hopeful. Jackie was still not responding, and chances of her recovering were becoming slim. There was nothing to do but wait. One more taxi and Sara was home.

It was nearly four in the morning. Sara lay awake in bed. Jackie had not turned up for jogging, and now she was gone. Maybe dead. She had begun dying hours ago, as Sara had run their regular jogging course in the cemetery. It had been Jackie's favourite place, of course, and she had no doubt appreciated the irony of the fact that Sara would be there, pushing herself toward some obscure goal as usual, while she tore her room apart and swallowed a bottle of pills.

It was a very exact loss, the loss of Jackie. It was as if she had been vacuum-sucked off the landscape. She would not come up the sidewalk to Sara's house any more, in her long narrow coat, her skirt fishtailing around her ankles. She would not puff behind her on the jogging route. And afterward, at dinner, she would no longer lay her charges against humanity. Charges that were impossible to counter, such as that one's mother had wasted her life and one's man friends were insensitive. Nevertheless, Sara always had argued against them, defending mankind, defending herself really, until finally Jackie would giggle, lay her precise small hand beside the teacup, and say, "Sara, don't worry. You're exempt. You're in my club."

What hadn't Jackie said to prepare for this night? Like a child walking into the forest, Jackie had dropped crusts behind her. In that soft, mocking voice she'd told Sara everything.

"When I'm depressed," she had said, washing dishes at the kitchen sink, "I can only sleep with the lights on."

"The lights have been on all night," the landlady had said over the din of party voices.

"I don't do so well, do I?" That one was across the table in a Chinese restaurant. "You'll have to pick up the pieces, Sara." "If I told you all the things I've done you wouldn't like me."

All the things she'd done. All the things she blamed other people for doing, in fact. Drunk and crying, there would be Jackie saying, "How many times can you do that to yourself before you're ruined for life?" She might have meant have an abortion or a destructive love affair; she might have meant fail to finish a poem or let down an editor who was counting on seeing her work. She might have meant just about anything. Only Jackie's delivery — the steady violet eyes, the tiny straight mouth, the righteousness that was part child, part methodist — made the melodrama convincing.

Jackie had always regarded herself with a certain fascination, as the only fruit in the garden without a worm. She detailed the spoilage around her, detailed its inroads on her own perfection. "I don't see how I can live my life," she would say, "when there's something wrong with everyone."

"What's wrong with me?"

"Nothing, Sara. You're my hero. I told you, I worship you."

"You've said that about people before, but you always find a flaw in the end."

"People let me down. I get disappointed in them."

"What disappoints you in me?"

"You're obsessed with having nothing get in your way."

Sara thought about that as she turned over in bed again. Did that mean she had failed Jackie by not letting anything — her, for instance — get in her way? In the way of what? They were not in a race. She swore it to the ceiling: they were not competing, they were not rivals. If Sara was ahead in her career, if she had sold a few stories to magazines, and there was a publisher waiting for her book, it meant nothing. Except perhaps that Jackie kept getting into scrapes and didn't get her work done. Sara had always thought Jackie was the more talented. Jackie was her friend. She loved Jackie; she needed Jackie. She did not need to win.

Finally, she fell asleep. It was more like waking, however. She went back twelve hours to her jogging, feeling the work of it, the sweat, the air on her skin.

She began by tying her shoe laces and shaking her wrists, and then she set off. The taller of the two friends, she was always in front when they ran, but it was more by privilege than by necessity. Hitting her stride, she missed the soft scrape of Jackie's feet behind her own spongy footfalls.

The road was wide and smooth. On either side, the sculpted lawns and huge trees waited, at this time of day dipped in the gilt of the late sun. Sara's milestones along the route would be the grave markers. Coming up, for instance, was Rebecca Coffin. She and Jackie had laughed at her, wife of Isaac Coffin, died in 1919. And there she was, her details written in shallow letters on soft marble and already eroding.

Past that and on Sara ran as she dreamed; she felt the fatique in her chest. She had gone this route so often, she could run it on a screen like one of those car-driving games where the road sped past. After the long curve and at the beginning of the straight diagonal across the centre of the cemetery, Sara looked over her shoulder, half expecting to see Jackie a hundred paces back, her hair bouncing on her shoulders the way it always did. Jackie ran like a sissy, her hands tiny ineffectual fists circling in front of her breasts, her knees turning inward. She could almost keep up, though: it was surprising. But she wasn't there. Even her ghost wasn't there. Well, thought Sara, commenting on her dream even as she dreamed it, if there's no ghost she can't have died yet.

And then Sara was into the hard part of the run, and the sun was slipping out of sight. Random rays shot out to make a last show, but already the cool damp rising from the ground insinuated itself around her ankles. Always at this point, she felt she couldn't make it. Her legs, her chest, even her arms were aching. Usually about now Jackie groaned and quit. Usually about now Sara would put on a burst and finish the course. In the dream she did just that, but it was harder without Jackie as audience.

And then she was lying in her bed and it was seven-thirty in the morning. By eight o'clock Sara was back at the hospital, where she sat for an hour in the waiting room outside Intensive Care. When the doctor finished his rounds, he came out to speak to her.

"I don't mind telling you now," he said, "that last night, it looked as if we were going to lose her."

Sara blinked.

"However, there's good news this morning. She's responding to pain."

Around noon, the parents arrived. Jackie's father squeezed one hand in a fist behind his back; her mother spoke in a whisper. He spoke to the doctors as if the issues were entirely in the terminology, as if there were no secrets that the machines could not break down, no burial so deep that medicine could not pull Jackie out of it. Sara watched them for the secret to what was wrong with their child: wasn't it their fault?

"I'm so ashamed," said Jackie's mother. "There's really nothing the matter with her, and she's taking up the doctor's time. The other people here are sick."

They sat in the waiting room and talked to a woman whose husband was eighty and had a stroke. The woman thought he had good colour that day. Neither Sara nor Jackie's mother mentioned the reason they had come. In the late afternoon, Sara left and went home to sleep. She called her office and Jackie's and made excuses. Then she fell into bed. The loneliness came back: Jackie would never return. She got up and took two aspirin, and then she began to dream. People died in the dreams, died in the middle of sentences they were uttering at dinner tables, died like dogs at Sara's feet. She did not believe the dreams while she had them. A part of her stood at the foot of the bed saying, Oh dear, another death dream, this is not very healthy. And then she went very deeply to sleep.

She was entering a room in her house, one that existed behind the closet door, one which she had not noticed before. There was a coffin there, that sinister shape that coffins were, narrow at the top and bottom, wider where the shoulders would be if there were a body inside. The box was covered with dirt. Sara understood that Jackie had buried herself alive and that it was her responsibility to dig with her fingers and get her out. With earth under her nails she lifted the lid, took Jackie out, and made her stand.

The girl was limp and boneless, but Sara was determined she should walk. She took her by the elbow. Jackie was like rags and rotting wood: she lurched, her mouth gaped, and she fell, finally pulling Sara down too. Then they were joyously under the surface of a clear stream, swimming. Jackie's hair streamed behind her, and Sara gulped hair, choked on it, so that when she woke it was because she thought her heart had stopped.

It was dusk again. She thought about jogging and decided against it. She called the hospital: no change. She didn't want to face Jackie's parents again, so she went out to dinner alone before going down to the hospital. But when she came out of the elevator in front of the Intensive Care unit, they were ready to step into it, on their way to a hotel.

Jackie's mother now regarded Sara with hostility. By this time they too must have got around to thinking about reasons, about blame. They looked as if they had decided that the secret lay in Sara, but they were too proud to ask.

Sara had been in the waiting room only a few minutes when the doctor came out.

"She's coming around. You can go in and see her."

Jackie was not quite conscious, but she had been moving. She'd pushed down the sheet to expose her bare chest. There was a tube in her nose and one in her stomach; blood was caked around her nostrils and lips. She had a big turquoise plastic umbilical cord in her mouth with steam bubbling in it. There was also a wire taped to her breast, a catheter in her arm, and something down her throat. The nurses told Sara they'd tied Jackie's arms to the sides of the bed so that she wouldn't knock the apparatus away. Sara saw Jackie's eyelids flicker, and a flood of gratitude went through her.

"Sit with her, if you like. Talk. Help her come out of it."

For hours, Sara sat by the bed, holding Jackie's cold hand and burbling as she would to a fussy baby.

"Jackie, you're waking up! It's so good to see you! Can you hear me? Can you? Can you see over there where the nurses are all sitting at their station? They look like a bunch of sparrows on a wire."

Jackie smiled at that: they often played simile games. Sara tried to keep going, but her friend groaned sometimes and twisted on the bed, thrusting herself backwards like a fish trying to escape the line that pulled it out of the dark. Jackie's eyes were closed, and her lips hardly moved, but she spoke.

"The world's gone mad," she said. And then, "Are you going to do a show about it?"

Sara pulled her hand back sharply. Shortly afterward, Jackie began to sob. The nurses asked Sara to leave so they could clean up the patient.

Sara went back to the cemetery. The iron gates were locked after dark, but there was a place where she could get one foot on a cement post and the other in a thick curl of iron. She swung over the top and dropped down into the dark on the other side. The city vanished as her feet hit the grass: the trees absorbed the skyline, and the lights of the houses close up against the stone walls only winked through the foliage. The deserted roads with their tick, tick, tick of a dotted yellow line gleamed faintly between charcoal shrub and inky ground. It was as if all life had been turned to ash there. The place was utterly dark, utterly sympathetic.

When she saw the light, Sara wanted to hide, but she was afraid to move. It was low to the ground and yellowish: it flickered. She'd read about corpses giving off phosphorescence, or was that the sea? The night was windless, the light the only moving thing. Sara took a few steps toward it. The light did not change.

Now she could see that it was coming from the foot of a gravestone. She could see the marble it reflected off and a dark wreath. Perhaps a hobo was warming himself at a campfire? But what sort of hobo would hang around a graveyard in the middle of the night? A hobo like herself. She did not wish to encounter such a one: it would be more frightening than meeting the dead.

Ten steps ahead and she could see that no one was there. The flame was a candle enclosed in a glass box, laid by some mourner on a fresh grave. She let her breath out and walked past the spot, over a mound and into a lower pasture of modest stones. Suddenly she was in a meadow of little flames. There must have been two dozen of them, each circled by a small sun which skimmed the dark earth. She stopped to read the names on the stones they lit. Foreign birthplaces, foreign expressions of loss spoke an awful loneliness. But the flames, as she looked over them, were a merry crowd; death was a joining, then, to the lost familiar.

But Jackie wasn't dead. The flames stirred, becoming frantic, as a wind passed over their boxes. Sara walked on into the older part of the cemetery, where the graves were not tended, where they were vast monuments grown over with ivy, idols to the idea of man or woman. Jackie wasn't dead, although she had tried to be. She had flubbed it. She had made an incomplete statement. She had made death a messy, halfway thing. If it was a kind of virginity to be alive, then Jackie, like her innocence, was tainted. Life would appear to come back to her, its vessel would not be intact. Something of it would have leaked away. Maybe part of Jackie's leg or her palm or her tongue would not come back. Maybe part of her brain would not come back. Maybe she would always be a little bit dead.

"So," said Sara out loud, "that's what you wanted. To muck up the absolutes some more. To turn one more thing into a fraud."

When Sara went to the hospital the next morning, Jackie had the tubes out and was sitting up in bed. The nurses had been combing her hair; it was spread out on her shoulders.

"Hi, Sara, what are you doing here?"

"We had a dinner engagement."

"Oh, no, did I ruin your evening?"

"Jackie, you must have known I'd come looking for you."

Jackie closed her lips in a pout. "I knew you would," she said, beginning to wail. "I thought you'd come around

8:30. But I thought that by then I'd be . . . well, it would all be finished."

You miscalculated, Sara thought. "I didn't get there till eleven," she said.

Something hard flashed in Jackie's eyes: *are you calling me a liar?* But she put out her arms to be hugged. "You saved my life!" The sweetness in her voice was gone; perhaps her throat was raw from the tube. "I must have scared you a lot," she said in the voice of one making amends.

"You mean you must have hated me."

"Oh no, not you, Sara. I'd never hate you. I *love* you."

Sara went out and cried in the toilet. All the things she wanted to say to Jackie and couldn't: *Next time, don't arrange to be rescued. Why choose me to do your dirty work? I'm not your servant. I'm not responsible for the remains.* Now that Jackie was alive, Sara felt like killing her.

There were two more days with Jackie in the hospital. Sara seethed at the arrogance of her friend, lying there disdainfully absorbing hundreds of dollars of medical assistance every hour, too polite to inform the doctors that they were making a mistake to bring her around, that she did not want to live. Because it was clear that Jackie still believed that the world had gone mad and people were faintly despicable for their participation in it. The psychiatrists gathered around and asked Jackie questions about how she felt: they took notes while she expounded. And what about me, Sara thought from the sidelines, what about me?

A New Start

A New Start

On New Year's Day the Bagel restaurant on College Street was the only place open for blocks. It was murder on hangovers: a wedge of surly faces plugged the doorway, and inside the waitresses cursed in the din. "Was that apple sauce or sour cream on the blintzes?" "Wait a minute, sir, I've only got two hands, all right?" But a small silence at a back table allowed a girl — she was really almost thirty but was small and often confused, and people thought of her as a girl, which she liked — to put down her cup with sudden elation.

"This is going to be a good year for me," she said. "I can feel it. My life goes in four-year cycles. Four years ago I had a good year. Now I'm going to have another."

"I think you should renegotiate your contract," said the man with her. He was a lawyer. "One in four isn't so hot." They had met three years ago. She was counting him in the low part of the cycle. "What was so great about four years ago?"

She squinted at the wall. "What was it? I just felt good. I was on my own, I guess. I'd left my husband, and everything was new all of a sudden."

She watched her second husband smile wanly across the table. He was older than she: he had also been married before. For three years now she had enjoyed the second debut of being his new, tender bride. But the night before, among his old friends, she had felt different. The way he stood beside her, dutifully, without looking in her face, had made her feel faded, lined, like a wife whom time more than desire enshrined. He had remarked sadly on the unattached women there, women his friends had cast off — it had been a big year for divorces — as if he felt a personal guilt. "Peggy darling," he said to her, "do you know that the thought of intimacy with another person terrifies me?"

That night, the first night of the new year, as they were preparing for bed, he became nervous. He put his robe over his jeans and paced between the bureaus. His wife was talking about a play she wanted to see.

"Becky White," he said, "told me it was no good."

The name stood up awkwardly in the bedroom. It was as if a giant stuffed doll had been introduced on a dance floor. Peggy excused herself to the doll and went to bed. Malcolm turned abruptly and walked out of the room.

When at last he joined his wife, she was lying on her back, awake.

"Malcolm dear," she said, "do you have something to tell me?" She hadn't *had* to say it. Once she had, the air around them contracted.

"I'm having an affair with Becky White."

The pain started instantly, shooting down through her breasts. Her stomach clenched, and her neck arched as if to expose the most vulnerable place and have it over with. Automatically, he put a protective arm across her chest. She groaned. The pain was very hot and drawn; finally it settled into the pelvis. He kept talking about which night it had been when the affair began and how he was so sorry and he'd always been bad for her anyway. He would move out right away. She should really forget him and get on with her own life. She'd be glad enough of it soon. He reminded her that she had thought it was going to be a good year.

But the pain was still burning in her lower abdomen, and she was thinking only of it, of what was happening in her body. Could she be having an orgasm? There were certainly similarities, but this was lasting longer.

Peggy worried about that hot sensation. Did it mean she was a masochist? In the opinion of her friends, she was not. She had simply experienced a severe trauma. She tried to put it out of her mind. But aside from her pain she did not have much to think about. It was all Malcolm's doing; she was only the recipient. Although Becky White the stuffed doll was just a prop, not really part of the drama, she did remain in the bedroom. Peggy had waves of nausea, imagining the exact moment of betrayal. Malcolm had taken this prop in his arms and kissed it. The nausea must have swept him too, hot and horrifying. For three years she and Malcolm had danced their dance, leaping up to each other's arms, catching the weight, feeling the bones shift under the other's skin. But then he had cut to someone else. The boards must have swum under his feet. A long kiss he'd given this Becky, a fast hand between the thighs, and then he'd led her off to a bed somewhere.

She went right off her food, thinking that way. She

would put down her fork after the first bite. "You were my feast, my nourishment," she said to her husband. "You've pinched me off, pinched off the cord," she told him. Her stomach shrank. She thought perhaps he would notice and find her thinness attractive. Because Malcolm was still around. He had plans to move out, but he had not actually done it. He sat at a table making lists of the furniture he would take and the furniture he would not take. She would move from chair to chair as he pointed first to one, then the other.

"You've polluted me. I'll be twisted and scarred." She felt she had been trusting and loyal when they met; now she would grow old like the others at the New Year's party, Malcolm and his friends. They were like the grey spires in a burnt-out forest, leaning on each other until one gave way and collapsed with a crash into the bog. She told him so.

"Go paint a picture," he said. "There's a lot of powerful imagery moving in you. You have an important life to lead."

She painted her wonderful street as a ghost street, windy, and her row of peaked houses empty at the top with broken gable windows where pigeons went in and out. The main floors were full of blue rooms where people squatted in front of flickering televisions. She painted her husband as a stone, a petrified stump near her front door. She was there beside the stone. She had squeezed the stone and banged on it and held it to her breast and cuddled it; it had sighed and turned over, but it was still a stone.

At last he was gone.

"It was no good," she said to her friends. "I wanted out anyway." That was a lie. The marriage may have been no good, but she would never have left. She had left one husband; she would not leave another.

There is something people say about deaths and separations. They say that one is left alone with one's memories. Peggy had almost been looking forward to this, expecting her memories to be better company than Malcolm. She sat on a sofa with a tea tray in front of her, staring at the thin shadows under the winter trees, waiting for her memories. But the memories would not sit down opposite and commune: there was revolt among them.

At the beginning, when they were falling in love, a hotel room in Paris. Hardly bigger than the bed in its centre. They had to get up by turns in the morning, wash and dress one at a time because there was not room for both of them to walk around. She would usually go down for breakfast first, in the slow elevator, saying bonjour to the Germans in the hallway, trying to read *Le Monde* while waiting for the café au lait. When he walked into the dining room, she would look up and smile. Once she looked up and did not know him. He came toward the table, and she panicked. She could not remember where she was. Was this her first husband? A trip with a friend? Was she going to marry again? This stranger? Only when he sat down did she realize that he had shaved off his moustache that morning.

She never told him about that. It was just a temporary jog in the memory, a filing error. Perhaps it had happened because they travelled so much, she and Malcolm. It was strange that they did; it was as if, disbelieving in their union, they wanted to impress it upon as much of the world as possible. In truth, Malcolm found travelling very difficult. He often wanted to go back to the room after breakfast and spend the morning reading.

Now she was remembering a beach in Vancouver, walking in pinkish sand, poking at shell chips with two long sticks he had found. He jumped up to a rock that was scalloped with the black lace of dying kelp; she remembered the rock perfectly. He brandished his stick. She began to fight with him; cross, cross, cross went the sticks. They moved in a circle around each other like pirates. One stick would break, its owner would be defenceless. They both knew this and played on. Peggy's broke.

She didn't like that memory. Surely there were happier ones. Where was the long line of pretty scenes she'd saved? It was breaking apart; she was frightened. Who would she be without this staff? She had been a Miss once, and a Mrs. someone else. She was Mrs. Leddy now and losing that would be too awful. She clung to Mrs. Leddy as to a stout log in a bad sea. Save me, save my memories, she cried.

Finally they had settled down in the house on Brunswick Avenue, the one she had lived in with her first husband, its red brick front squashed between two larger ones, a turret popping out the top. The house had always made her think of her mother. When she was younger she had pestered her mother for stories. "Tell me about your wedding," she would say, and then, "What did your first house look like?" She happened to know that her parents' first house had been on Hochelaga Street in Regina and that it also had been red brick, with gables. Knowing that had meant something to her as a child. Now no one would ever ask her about this house. They never asked about the first husband, certainly, she was used to that. Now they wouldn't ask about the second. What would they ask about? Her whole life was becoming unmentionable. She wanted her memories to matter.

"We once stayed a week in this marvellous cabin in northern Ontario," she said out loud. "There was a river beside it, which froze. We had skates — no, we had to borrow them from the landlord, that's right — and we went out for miles on the ice.'' At such places there are only a few days of perfect skating each year. The ice might melt and refreeze with bumps in it, or the snow would cover it too quickly; something was bound to go wrong. But they had three perfect days in which they skated along the river for miles. Skated as people skate in dreams, along a narrow, shining band of ice that slid between white mounds and black trees and under little bridges. At the bridges they had to step over the edge to walk around in the snow because the ice underneath was weak.

She was smiling now. That one was a nice memory to have, a pearl remaining when the string had broken, and all the others had rolled under chairs. She was grateful to have this one perfect thing left. She made the perfect memory into a large picture book, and she turned the pages to see how far she could go. There he was, pulling off her skates with his own hands. He had taken her to stand by the fire afterward and had whispered in her ear. It had been so cold in their room they went to bed in their clothes and undressed under the covers. He had always had a very warm body. He had loved her then. Or at least so she had believed. She dropped sideways on the sofa and began to cry.

This was Malcolm's real betrayal; he had turned these memories into such treacherous things. She was furious at her need for his fidelity to keep her past beautiful. She hated her pain She must be free. She would take a knife to the memories if she had to, gouge and shred them. They'd always fought, especially on holidays. He hated to do the slightest little thing for her. After they made love he'd drop instantly into a dead sleep, and she would lie awake, lonely. Who knew, probably he'd been deceiving her all along. Becky Whites were everywhere, and he'd only told her when he did because he was tired of being married. He had a rotten temperament anyway; she could remember her inward groan on mornings when he looked up from sleep with that scowl.

But no, he was sweet! An alarmed chorus of little voices erupted. Don't do this thing to us, your own darlings!

Peggy sighed deeply. Stay quiet, she said, I won't destroy you after all. In truth she hadn't the strength to cancel the lovely past, the only one she had. She hadn't the strength to survive brand new and empty until someone else came along and filled her up again. She had done that with her first husband. Yes, she remembered the intoxicating clarity of the year of the fresh start. But she would not do it again. You get one round free, but the next one counts. It can't be swept off the record. Nothing can be repeated, not even a new start.

When her husband began to come back to visit her, she was cool. There were, however, moments of tenderness. Once she asked him about the week in the cabin in the snow.

"Remember skating on the river?"

"Yes."

"Wasn't it beautiful then?"

"Beautiful," he said, "we were so happy."

"Remember the way the ice separated from the bank and the dangerous foot or two of water that we had to step over?" In fact he had always slipped in and got his feet wet, perhaps because he was heavier than she was.

"Remember when the dog went out into the middle of the pond?"

Oh God, she did remember! There had been two dogs at the cabin. The collie was not very smart, perhaps it had been overbred. It walked out to the middle of the pond where the river widened and the ice was thin. She had looked out the kitchen window and saw the dog, only its head and forepaws visible, treading water. The older dog, the smart one, sat by the edge of the pond watching calmly.

Peggy and Malcolm had run for their boots. Malcolm called the collie, but he wouldn't come; he kept turning toward the far shore, pawing the thin ice around him, making the hole bigger and bigger. The water was terribly cold, and the collie was tiring himself, getting nowhere.

They had pushed a plank toward him on the ice, but it wouldn't go nearly far enough. Malcolm got down on his stomach and tried to worm himself across the ice, but it had begun to crack. She shouted at him to come back. He tried to stand, and then he was up to his waist in water. So Peggy had rescued him, and he had run into the house for dry clothes before he froze. Alone she'd been able to attract the dog's attention. She had reached a rock near the shore and leaned out over the ice and had persuaded him to come toward her, breaking the ice in his way until she could reach his collar.

"I remember dragging that dog out of the water," Malcolm said, shaking his head. "I was soaked."

But no, Peggy said to herself. You were inside changing your boots. *I* rescued the dog. I did. She looked at Malcolm, the light in his eyes as he recalled his adventure, and smiled. "Yes," she said, "I remember too."

After Easter Malcolm came back for good. He knocked at the door at midnight on Saturday, and Peggy let him in. He didn't ask her to, but she forgave him, too. Sometimes she wondered why he had come back. Certainly it was not to save her; perhaps it was to put his own memories in order. Perhaps Becky White turned him out; perhaps that was all there was to it.

By summer's end the separation was beginning to seem like nothing more than an interlude, a bout of disease, something tropical caught on a holiday that had seized them and shaken them hard and had been sweated out at last. The backward knitting-up had begun, and Peggy could reminisce on those hours she'd spent looking out the window.

"Remember," she would say to herself, sitting with her tea, fingering the past as if it were a rosary, "remember when I thought he didn't love me anymore and I cried all afternoon? Remember when he left me for Becky White?"

The Independent Woman

The Independent Woman

The others had given up on Lasha when she rushed to the turnstile, waving, her legs flashing under a thin cotton skirt. She shouted to the ferryman, but he went on hoisting the gangplank, implacable. Then she stopped, dropped her arm and brushed her hair back from her face.

"Lasha!" a woman called from the upper deck of the boat.

"You're leaving without me!" The latecomer pointed to the clock hanging over the waiting area and shook her head. She was alone on the dock with ten feet of water between her feet and the ferry for Hanlan's Point.

"Get the next one over to Centre Island and walk over. Look for the Blickers, they missed it too."

Lasha nodded and turned away. The boat began to move off, and she was instantly part of the backdrop.

"I'm glad she came alone." The voice that had called from

the deck was a husky one, a voice which gave the tone of slander to all it repeated. Those for whom the comment was intended nodded. They were also glad. None of the group gathered for the picnic liked Lasha's lover, whom they classified as a brooder. "You have to watch these brooders," they said. "They don't talk much, but they're dangerous." The group moved away from the edge to sit down, leaving only one, Peter, with his foot on the rail, staring down into the water.

Peter supposed this meant that Lasha was on her own again. He had predicted that the affair would be over by fall. It was the last week in August now, and already the sticky heat felt nostalgic. It was the worst time of year in Toronto, and the optimist in him always wished to go off to the bush country and build a cabin. But it had been twelve years since he'd escaped a city August, and then it had only been to work in London, which was no better.

Looking at the still water, Peter thought how unappetizing the harbour was, with bits of wood and bubbles flecking the surface. He'd been to Britain again this year, and every trip he made served to remind him that his home was small, unimportant and colonial; that his status here was therefore suspect, as his commitments here were less commitments than inertia. Or so he felt until he'd been back long enough to regain his bearings. The only way to live here was to embrace it, to believe that it was the only place in the world.

The ferry throbbed inside itself. Peter turned his back to the water and leaned on his elbows on the rail, watching the group. Lasha's friends: like her, they were in their late twenties, fifteen years his junior, ambitious neophytes in television, theatre, publishing. They begged to be recognized, even this evening as they headed away from the city for a picnic dinner, but the other passengers on the ferry were oblivious. In this city there were always fifty or a hundred ambitious new talents breaking onto the scene. They did, finally, although not in the way they expected. They would fill the vacancies when their predecessors dropped out or were dropped; they wouldn't change anything, although they all believed they could. He looked back at them in sympathy. He used to feel his photographs would do more than make people want what they didn't have. He still believed himself a little different than most: even now he wasn't prepared to admit this was all there was. Lasha had reminded him of that specialness in himself. He could have had her, he thought. Could still.

A woman came toward him. He swung his left arm open.

"Isn't it great to be out on the water?"

Peter hugged her and felt momentarily fresh and undamaged. That was the point of these girls, the lovely young ones. There were so many and he could have his pick. It had been that way for years, and it was wonderful while it lasted, but he often thought they'd have their revenge on him in time. He turned away from this one, Valerie, to look at the island looming near, a mirage. It was as flat as a plate spun off the mainland, just a low rim of grass with a film over it, a fine silver mist. It looked newborn.

The four of them thudded down the gangplank – husky-voiced Anne and her husband, Roger, pulling a bundle buggy loaded with provisions, himself and Valerie. The ferry made its backward exit, leaving an insulated quiet tugged at only by water birds. Behind them, the city looked like an untidy pile of toys. Ahead was the point. A paved path led the picnickers away from the dock to a fantasyland of lawn bordered by tall, tassled grasses and whip-like tree sprouts whose leaves dangled as weightless silver. And then there were the trees, century-old willows. They raised their elegant spray higher than the now-distant bank edifices and dropped their foliage thick as petticoats just inches above the ground. They stood like the governesses of any man's dreams, and the soft white mist clung to them.

Peter fell in behind the leaders on the way to the fire pit. Sensitive to beauty, he'd stopped taking pictures at times like this; he preferred to participate. He dropped his leather bag, took off his jacket and jammed it in with his jogging clothes. Then he rolled up the sleeves of his worn Levis shirt. He looked boyish. It was his stock-in-trade, this boyishness, his thick dark hair that could have been shaped by a bowl, his gangly legs. With the bag thrown over his shoulder, he had a hand free for touching Valerie.

The site Anne and Roger had in mind was past the tennis courts, past the open meadow, past all the other visitors. Only when they arrived at a small beach sheltered by bushes and isolated by its position midway between Centre Island and the Hanlan's Point ferry docks, did Anne call a halt. They all dropped what they carried to unpack the food and gather kindling, all but Valerie who went down to the water to kick sand.

"There come the Blickers, with Lasha."

Peter looked up. The late members of the group had made the long walk from the opposite direction quickly. Lasha was out of breath. Her face seemed blurred, her cheeks flushed, and the strawberry blonde strands of hair across her throat a fine wash against steady blue eyes. She was sturdier than he remembered.

"Lasha!" He opened his arms for her to leap in. She

didn't quite, but held with a peculiar tension to his shoulders. "How was your summer?"

"Wonderful, wonderful." She pushed away from him and looked for his eyes. "I got some terrific work done."

Arms around each other's waist, they turned away from the group. Peter looked back over his shoulder. The Blickers were blaming each other for the fact that they'd missed the ferry. More beer came out of the bags, and Valerie came up from the beach to demand that someone swim with her.

"It was a great summer all around," Lasha was saying, "but the new man and I are through."

"I predicted that," he said.

Bloody bastard, thought Lasha. She drew away from Peter and watched him fidget. Only a year ago she'd thought she was in love with him. She still longed for him and then felt disappointed when she saw him. He was too quick; he was callous. But she gave in to a wave of affection as he peered from under his forelock and told her all about Valerie. She was always forgiving Peter. And for what? One felt that the *real* Peter was sensitive and good and discriminating, despite the scant evidence given by his actions.

This was not the first time Lasha had watched him go through a romance with one of her friends. It had hurt at first, then it had made her angry, but now she viewed a new affair with tolerance, the way others viewed her own, perhaps. This bunch was a set of bodies, of faces, that remained loosely bound by some unclear affinity: you chose one, that was your pig in the middle for a time, then he or she went back to the rim and you chose another. Right now, for instance, there was Valerie, kicking sand, taking a long drag on a joint and eyeing Peter and Lasha.

Briefly, Lasha pitied her friend. Peter was perverse: he flirted with Lasha now, long after he'd had his chance and left her for someone, anyone, else. It was always that way when she went out alone. Other women's men came on to her. But when she was in a couple, she was ignored, not of interest — like Valerie. Lasha liked it better this way, being alone. She had the power in her own hands. She laughed gaily at something Peter said. In the middle of her laugh, Valerie shouted and he went to her.

Covering her blush with a hand to her hair, Lasha looked around for someone to talk to. The Blickers were one of the very few permanent couples. Barb Blicker was the kind of woman who felt unworthy of a dinner party if she hadn't cooked at least one course. Tonight she was pulling a cake out of her bag. Jack gazed at her across the grass and said so quietly that only a spouse of a decade or a professional eavesdropper like Lasha could have heard, "Barb, you're over-excited."

"And it's getting awfully dark for your sunglasses," she retorted without looking up. A tender marital jibe. Lasha had to turn her head, the tears came up so fast. Bloody bastard, she thought, and this time her lost lover was in her mind. She would not cry over this one. It *was* getting dark, actually. The greens of the grass and the lake, thirty feet away through the trees, were flattening to a slate blue. The waves were rising like a crowd, irrationally, because there was no wind. Sky, water, and ground were losing their distinction. For comfort, Lasha moved near Jack Blicker.

"Terrible living with Barb, really," he said with a sideways smile. "It's left me so useless about cooking. She does it so well, I haven't learned a thing." They both watched Barb help set up the tables. Jack had taken off his sunglasses. They hung on his chest.

"A silver chain for your sunglasses! Isn't that a bit pretentious?"

"He loses things," Barb piped up in his defence. "Every Christmas I tell my mother to send him a pair of brown driving gloves. Every March he loses them."

"And I bet your mother put your mittens on a string around your neck," Lasha said to Jack. Any couple made her want to do that, to nuzzle between them, sharing the affection.

Two white linen tablecloths came from the depths of the bundle buggy: as they were spread on the picnic tables, the site was transformed. Three bottles of Mumms came out next and were stood on the white stretch in the twilight, pink foil tops twinkling wickedly. Pale marbled meat lay on wax paper awaiting the fire. A feast was materializing. Everyone agreed it was nothing short of magic. Standing in a circle, the guests watched Roger strip the foil, untwist the wire, and aim the bottle into the trees. Lasha always jumped before the pop.

There were loud hurrahs, and now the champagne was caught in the basin of her plastic glass. Lasha drank the bubbles, feeling the tiny pain as each died on her tongue. Peter migrated toward her under the trees. With glasses in hand, they picked through the undergrowth toward the water, leaving behind the voices that said, "Fire ready?" "Five minutes." "Find the tongs, will you?"

Lasha stumbled on a root. Peter caught her arm, and champagne splashed all over her wrist. In the sand her heels sank with each step until she took off her shoes. Then she was shorter, and the sand dragged her backwards.

Ahead of them was the water and the sun setting, the coast of the United States. They made a little nest for sitting and dug holes in the sand to take their glasses. Lasha gathered her skirt in her fingers and held it at her ankles.

"Do you see that?" Peter's voice was hushed. ("What do you see?" It was a game they used to play, lying on their backs in bed, sharing the visions that came up behind closed eyes in the darkness.) But their eyes were open; it was the sunset this time. Pink and bronze squared beams poured through the scrim of city air. The orb itself seemed to be sliding backwards, raking the sky as it went.

"I see a runner with a flare — no, it's just a flower-bed." Lasha sipped her small remaining amount of champagne. "What do you see?"

"Oh, never mind. You're too good at this now."

They talked about his work, her broken heart. "I refuse to let it bother me," said Lasha. "I'm over it."

Peter flung out his arms in awkward abandon. "Oh well, my dear," he said. "I thought you took up with him in rather indecent haste. I began to wonder if you ever really loved me."

Did he cling like that to the other women he'd hurt? Lasha thought of the catch of breath she used to feel, seeing him walk toward her and knowing that in one minute she'd be inside that embrace. It had always been more show than force, still, she wanted it.

"I hear you're a reformed man now with Valerie," she said.

"I was so fed up when I left for Britain this year," he said, avoiding the subject. "I walked all over London, saw all the places I used to go. It's not what it used to be. I wouldn't live there again; in fact, it made me realize why my ancestors emigrated."

"And Valerie?"

"We wrote. She was here when I got back. It's still good, you know."

The sun sank by inches, and as it did the sand seemed to rise around them and grow whiter. A voice came up behind in the silence.

"I'm going swimming before we eat, even if I have to do it alone." Valerie stepped around to place herself directly in front of them. She took off her sandals, unbuttoned her blouse, and drew her skirt over her head. As she dropped it, Peter moaned. Valerie stuck her tongue out at him. Then she stepped out of her panties and paraded to the water, digging her feet into the sand.

There was no point pretending either she or Peter were looking at anything else; Lasha sat for another minute, then got to her feet and brushed off the sand. Valerie shouted from the waves, and Peter picked up her towel and ran to catch her in it as she came back into the air. They waited for her to dress, and then the three of them walked back to where the table waited, flat white in the deepening dark.

The guests sat four on one side and three on the other. They passed pickles and rolls with sweet butter and two kinds of salad. There was red wine to go with the chops and the sausages. They were short of forks, so Jack and Barb had to share, but there was nothing else amiss. The picnic, they thought, was perfect.

"Candles," said the throaty voice of the hostess. "My God we forgot candles. How could we? Look how dark it's getting."

"She was from New York," Lasha was saying, her own voice rising on an alcohol bubble high in her throat. "She said, well, if it's going to be this flat all the way to Calgary, I'm going to have lunch."

"Do you see the tomatoes?" said Peter, leaning over Lasha's right shoulder.

"Peter, don't interrupt, I'm telling a story." He leaned the other direction then, but Lasha could feel him listening. "The thing that's funny," she said, "is that there *is* this fantastic Chinese restaurant in Calgary . . ."

"I don't see the tomatoes anywhere. It's so terribly dark."

"You'll have to run that by me again, about the train. I lost you somewhere."

The last pink beams of the sun had disappeared. The sky and the water were battleship grey and the grass had the glaze of pearls. Faces vanished and reappeared with cigarettes in front of them. Suddenly everyone was listening to Lasha's story about the Chinese restaurant and the lady from New York.

"I can't," she said to Jack. "I can't remember. There's no point to the story." Lasha was making everyone laugh, but the attention confused her. She wondered what they would all be saying if she weren't there and poured herself more wine.

"When does the last ferry go?" Lasha came to the surface, with Barb's cake untouched in front of her.

"Ten o'clock. But we called the water taxi for midnight — don't worry."

"I have to meet someone at eleven," she said. Lasha had learned to leave these parties before the end, before things became ugly.

People were discussing holidays in the sun. Then they were discussing someone's boyfriend who had come to stay and made indiscreet noises while making love. Barb laughed. Her husband told her she was out of control. Lasha wished someone would say that to her.

Out of the thick mist where the island let in a channel of lake water from the west appeared a double-decker ferry, coloured lights strung along its length, spraying chords of live jazz into the mist. The music and the sound of voices came as if on air toward the dinner table. The picnic fell silent.

"Just like in a Fellini movie," said someone.

"You mean Buñuel."

"Those awful singles cruises," murmured Anne. "They're getting panicky now, you see. It's nine-thirty and they haven't found Mr. Right."

Lasha felt her gorge rise. She stood. "You know, Anne," she said, "you are very brutal." She didn't care if Anne was the hostess.

People didn't speak for a minute. Lasha wondered how this picnic looked to the people on the cruise. The long chalky table top, the empty bottles of drink gathered at one end, the ashen red of the fire pit. Wet lips, dull ring-stones; the picnic had a kind of eyeless elegance.

"If we had a chandelier . . ." she started.

Valerie stood up and moved down the table near Lasha. She waved at the boat as it drew slowly opposite them, huge, only a hundred yards away across the grass.

"Hello, hello, look at us," Valerie shouted. She grabbed Lasha's hand.

"We are all rather drunk," remarked Lasha.

"Take your skirt off," Peter said. "You two, both of you." He steered the two women side by side toward the boat. "Take off your clothes and run over there to give the tourists a nice surprise." Valerie and Lasha did not look at each other. It was time to leave the table.

Wood for the bonfire had been delivered as ordered and stood in a low pyramid beside the pit at the edge of the sand. The group moved in a cluster to the beach, and Lasha went to the edge of the water alone. It was lighter there. There must be a moon somewhere, in cloud, she realized; it was reflecting back at her from the shallows. The waves came grey-green and full. Some looked as high as her thighs before they broke, and white poured from their crest. There was still no wind.

The moon is making those waves, thought Lasha. Pulling the water like a magnet pulling iron filings. She was reminding herself of something she'd been taught in school, something she believed in. Jack and Barb Blicker disappeared together into the brush down the beach; their shadows were darker green shapes. Peter and Valerie hugged beside her. Anne and Roger were cleaning up. The tiny flame of the bonfire made them huge. There were faint shouts and a bass throb on the air as the singles' ferry rounded the point and began to return. She wanted to do something extreme with her body — run, leap, wrestle. To be overpowered.

"Ready to swim?" Valerie again. Lasha looked up. There was trouble with the fire. Was the wood not dry enough? Perhaps a wind was coming off the lake. The blaze did not merit huddling around, and the party was in danger of dissipating.

"Swimming, that's the thing," said Anne in a tone of authority. Her voice still carried, even near the waves.

Lasha could only hear the beginnings of other people's sentences. The coffee had gone down fast, and the brandy bottle was empty. Peter was talking about Italian food, it seemed. The others were a blur. The grass, the switch-like little trees that might have been the crests of giant trees buried a hundred feet under the sand, the water, everything around her was moving.

"I'm going swimming."

Stepping backwards, she passed Peter: he reached out in the darkness and stroked her hip. Then she nearly collided with Jack and Barb returning from their tryst and said goodbye to them without knowing why. She giggled. On the far side of the fire where no one was looking, she took off her blouse and skirt, putting them in a heap under a bush. As she tucked her underwear under the pile, one of the men ran by, naked, his buttocks bright as a horse's in the dark.

"Beat you down there."

Lasha let him beat her. She walked to the water. When she met the waves they did not shock her skin; the water felt warm as flesh. It seemed to calm itself, settling around her as she slipped in. And the wave slept on the breast of the fish, she thought.

Peter had seen Lasha walk slowly toward the waves, her top half swaying in that inquisitive, bird-like way, her legs striking into the sand. He and Valerie got up seconds later. He was reluctant to strip, but she did it so aggressively that he had no choice. Valerie was stoned. She leapt ahead of him with knees high, breaking the waves, glistening white in a sliver of moonlight she seemed to have captured all for herself. At the moment when the water hit her pubic hair, she turned to look at him, gave an exhilarated little cry, and lay backward on the water. Peter made his way after her, careful of stones. The waves met him in the gut. He was knocked down, felt ridges of sand on the bottom, like the roof of a mouth, and then found his feet. Valerie climbed on his back.

When he looked around, their pathetic bonfire was on the left instead of the right.

"Jesus, we're drifting. There's some kind of current." He stood up in the water and walked back toward the fire, the waves beating at his knees, dragging the smiling Valerie through the waves. The moon slipped again and he saw where the others were standing waist-high in the water. Barb reached for his hand. They pulled themselves into a straight line, all of them, looking out at the grey masses of the water, the starless sky, and two moons, one above, one beneath the waves. The waves had turned from grey to clear black. The mist was going, and the city appearing at their backs again. Somehow after all this, they were friends, people who lasted for one another. One had to love people, thought Peter. He felt very young. All things are possible.

"Where's Lasha?"

There were six of them in the line. The moon revealed crest after crest of incoming waves, and behind the swimmers the water slid away from the sand.

"You call, Anne, your voice carries."

"Lasha! Wouldn't it be like her to disappear now, to just go for the ferry and make us worry."

Peter dropped the hands he held. He cursed himself for forgetting her, as if he had uncreated her by letting her drop from his mind.

"Didn't anyone bring a light?"

He ran out of the water and along the beach past the fire, looking in the trees and on the shore. He could not see her clothes; that was a good sign. He dressed faster than the others did and ran the mile and a half to the docks. All along the path he expected her to step out from the bushes and call his name.

They made a telephone call from the pay booth, and when the police launch came, they were almost sober. They had missed the last ferry, and the dock men had gone home. There was no way of knowing yet whether Lasha had been on it. Valerie began to sob hysterically. Trailing backwards through the water, looking at the wake left by the launch, the rest sat quite still while Anne complained about Lasha's pranks.

The Garden

The Garden

[illegible] a [illegible] [illegible] [illegible] [illegible] with [illegible] the [illegible] [illegible] [illegible] [illegible]. [illegible] [illegible] [illegible] [illegible] and [illegible] [illegible] with [illegible] [illegible]. In the [illegible] [illegible] [illegible] [illegible] [illegible] [illegible] [illegible] [illegible] the plants had [illegible] placed [illegible] [illegible] and [illegible] the [illegible].

All [illegible] he [illegible] [illegible] a [illegible] and [illegible] [illegible] [illegible] of [illegible] that would [illegible] of these [illegible]. So he went to the [illegible] of a [illegible] and [illegible]. [illegible] a [illegible] in a [illegible]

The Garden

Knew a man once, wanted to be a sheik. He went into business. He bought fine, well-lit premises, and made a restaurant. Bronze-tinted mirrors, hanging ferns, tropical trees, batik curtains. Round marble-topped tables and chairs with heart-shaped seats. In the corners, marsh-mallow couches for lovers. He made narrow, winding pass-ageways to a back lounge where tiny booths were tucked against the wall in almost total darkness, and the plants had to be replaced with dried branches and feathers. It was all very beautiful, and even the menu looked mysterious.

When it was decorated, he set out to staff his restaurant. He wanted a man for head waiter and eight women to be waitresses and barmaids. He had a clear vision of the perfect people; he thought of advertising, but decided that would bring in too many of the wrong sort. So he went to the manager of a personnel agency. He sat opposite the man at a big wide desk and in a few words described his needs. Then the businessman went back to his office in his restaurant and waited.

Soon they began to arrive. In their cloth coats with fur collars, their high suede boots, their leather shoulder bags, their best dress for interviews. They came into his office one by one, stretching their gloves off each finger separately, and he told them to sit. He asked them one or two questions about their working experience, but he said it wasn't important. He asked them to walk to the door and back.

It was not talent he was looking for; it was, he supposed, a demeanor and style that would speak well of his establishment. Classy was a little crass, but it was something like that he wanted. A girl with a patent leather belt over her coat he eliminated immediately. One who had waitressed before in a diner and had a loud voice, he dismissed with quick distaste. He looked at the hair, the scarves, the way they sat.

Then he met one who seemed to him just perfect. She was tall and small-wristed. She had long dark hair, tied neatly behind her head as a ballet dancer would wear it, with just a few wanton wisps over the ears. She had pale, flat, perfect features and she spoke laconically but with excellent grammar. He loved her. As she spoke about having been a receptionist, he closed his eyes and saw her in his restaurant, moving among the potted trees with a half-smile, acknowledging but not really seeing the patrons. He hired her. He telephoned the manager of the agency and told him that this woman, Jane, was just the right sort.

After that the women arrived less frequently, but they were rather more suitable. He hired two who looked remarkably like Jane — one was a redhead, but of the same build and personality, and the other was shorter, with a small, tightly coifed head and perfect pearly features. He

loved them both as soon as they said they would start Monday. He called the personnel man. The last two were great, he said, you're getting the idea. Get me five more.
The businessman envisioned his three women — Jane, Shelagh, and Sharon — in his new place, subtle and luminous, and he became even more scrupulous about hiring. By the end of the week he had six and decided to begin with them rather than hire any who were less than perfect. He asked them all to come in Monday morning to discuss things. Then he went home to rest.

All day Saturday and Sunday he worried about the head waiter he hadn't hired. He'd seen only a few men when he was interviewing, and he had rather lost interest. Now he knew he must find someone to do the job, but to tell the truth, he felt just a little proprietary about his waitresses. He wasn't happy about giving them over to another man. But he couldn't do the job himself. And a woman wouldn't do, not even a platinum-haired, pencil-thin matron. Just before he retired Sunday night, he thought of a solution. He called a friend, even though it was late, and said did he know any unemployed actors — his friend managed a theatre group — who were looking for a job. Preferably homosexual? Of course he did.

The next morning, just before the girls were to arrive, a man turned up at the restaurant. He was terribly thin, with hips like a ten-year-old girl's, a pile of tangled hair leaning over his brow, transparent skin, and a slight stutter, or at least a hesitation in his speech which sounded faintly foreign. The businessman wanted to ask, but he felt a little shy about it. He looked instead at the actor's long, greenish fingers and his full lips; he observed the way the man seated himself, his long legs together and the sharp hips twisted slightly to the side. His name was Cliff. Cliff solved the dilemma by saying he would not give the manager any trouble by pursuing the waitresses, as he was not interested in women. The businessman hired him on the spot, but he had a warmish feeling of discomfort, as if something about himself were too obvious, and he had been understood by this man in a way he did not understand himself.

It was a long time before things ran smoothly in the restaurant, for the women and Cliff were only part of it; there was the cook and the equipment and the ordering and the bar to be attended to. There were failures of the soufflés, soapy eruptions from the dishwater and the pouring of over-generous drinks, to name a few crises. The businessman was harassed; he doubted it would all come together for the official opening.

His one source of pleasure was the bevy of waitresses, who continued to be perfect. He'd called them together and seen them as a group, six beautiful women standing demurely before him. At first meeting they had looked at each other quietly with a hint of amusement, for the six might have been sisters. They were like a string of convent girls, and seductive. He asked Jane, who seemed preeminent by the fact that she was the mould from which the others had been cast, to arrange for outfits; he did not wish to interfere. They had left him, chattering about what they might wear.

Now the restaurant was open. The waitresses moved peacefully, without complaint, among his hanging lamps and flowers. They blushed in their long jersey skirts and smooth, dove-coloured tops. They smiled at each other and at him. They seemed to like the businessman; this mattered a great deal to him, and he was happy. It was only after the business had been operating for some weeks and gaining patrons daily that the businessman felt restless. As Jane slid past him carrying a plate of escargot, he suddenly thought — she's too perfect, she isn't real.

He began to watch her. She was really very beautiful, he thought, as he saw her lean down over the marble table, her breasts rising to meet their milky reflection in the smooth surface. She straightened and turned away, her spine rising alongside the slim curving stem of his tropical birch tree. The shadows made her tawny, yet he could imagine the pallor of her skin under the costume he had bought for her. And then he felt it; the pit of his stomach rose up like a wave. That which had been hidden for these busy weeks crested and broke. Desire seemed to move the leaves above him and bring sweat to stand out under his shirt.

While the businessman watched Jane, he noticed Cliff watching him with a reproving coolness. He saw that his spying on her was not something a manager of a restaurant should do. His stalking became more covert and more exciting.

Exploiting dim corners and the angles of mirrors to discover his prey, he saw that, like a timid forest animal, she was aware of him. She camouflaged herself. He had seldom been required to be subtle: his were the most obvious and acceptable of needs. Now when he descended to this netherland he found that Jane was there before him. She avoided each approach without seeming to notice it. When his gaze dreamt unfocussed on an inch of her forearm, the skin seemed to flicker in recognition. Wariness increased his lust until it was almost unbearable. A chance sight of her whispering hips as she swung them lightly to one side, arms high holding a tray of cocktails, made his abdomen curl.

He was imprisoned. His unrelieved excitement confined

him to that establishment; it made his limits that woman. This made him angry. She had all this power; her shyness seemed to him its most cruel exercise. He decided to relax his authority over the waitress, to ignore their roles, and to approach her. He did not demean himself by this tendering to an employee, for inside him, as hard as a bead of silver, he carried the knowledge — that assurance he'd had even as a teenager snapping his fingers at women on the street to make them look at him, merely so he could bask in their tired acknowledgement — that such tendering was yet another humbling of her, another proof of his power.

He began to expand the smile he addressed to Jane, allowing it to linger, to flick lightly down to her lips. Her eyes shifted. He opened his lips a little; he let his eyes drift down from her face. Her eyes moved away more deliberately. He was accustomed to such defence, encouraged by it. He imagined himself lifting the folds of her heavy, soft skirt, lowering himself under it, spending his heavy pulse on her under the ferns and the mirrors. Passing her in the narrow hall to the dark cloisters at the back of the restaurant, he allowed himself one word, so soft it might only have been a breath. He watched over his shoulder; her back elongated, and she turned the corner with a twist of her head. It didn't matter. He was elated with his lust.

Days later, she stood before the full-length mirror in the entrance, knotting a silk scarf around her neck, ready to leave work at nine o'clock. He saw that no other girls were in sight and approached her from behind. He extended a finger and drew it slowly down the top of her lifted right arm.

"Going home?" he murmured.

"No."

The finger momentarily stopped. A come-on? Or did she have an engagement? He let his hand fall off the point of her elbow and lifted it to the back of her neck, but she pulled the scarf around briskly so that he touched silk instead of skin. He dropped his hand to her shoulder and let it lie there, warmly, with a certain weight behind it. His thighs tightened.

"A girl like you has to be careful," he murmured. Even he was aware that he sounded sleazy as a pimp.

She turned away from his cool spectre in the mirror and addressed him with the cutting edge of her profile, "So it seems." She was mocking him.

After that he withdrew to rethink his manoeuvres. He hung around his girls, filing his nails or peering into the drawers of linen, composing a bored look, and listening. For the first time it seemed to him odd that the women did not talk of their private lives, not in his hearing at least. He only had a part of their lives in his restaurant: his waitresses walked the streets as free women sixteen hours a day and two full days a week. He felt he'd woken accidentally to a group infidelity; his women belonged to other men — worse, to themselves — behind his back. He pouted, he alluded to "after hours" activities, he withdrew into hurt formality. All to no avail. The women, trained to behave graciously regardless of his mood, trained to act as if they were oblivious to his mood, were in fact oblivious.

A curious thing happened then. The businessman's ardour for Jane evaporated. He realized it with astonishment one day as he watched her tally drinks, leaning on an elbow at the slippery black bar, her long neck arched over it like a branch over a midnight stream. It frightened him. He retreated to his office to examine the absence of lust. Self-doubt assailed him. What could be wrong? He concluded it was Jane's hardness, her plastic imperviousness that snuffed him.

Meanwhile the restaurant had begun to do well. Patrons

returned, bringing their best clients to lunch under his birch trees. In the cocktail hours salespeople lingered over drinks, and late, late at night at the back corners bare-shouldered women let drift their smoky breath, silent as watchmen at the rise of the moon. He came in by eleven each morning and never left before 2:00 A.M. The streets outside had begun to seem superfluous. He lived in the rarified tropic of his restaurant; his previous personal life was the least significant of his endeavors. He encouraged his friends to come to the restaurant, for he had no inclination to go to other places.

But he needed outside activity, especially after losing interest in Jane. He called a woman he knew and arranged to — what? Not to go out to dinner. To drive to a country inn and theatre, he supposed. He didn't enjoy the date. He disliked the woman's loud voice and the stiff chic of her white linen pants.

Even before this failed engagement, the businessman had felt curiously drawn to Shelagh, the red-haired woman whom he'd hired mostly for her resemblance to Jane. She was in truth rather different, in texture if not in contour. Her skin was transparent and lightly freckled, giving her a shifting surface, like a shallow stream in sunlight. The angles of her collar bones protruded, and he could detect the corners of hip bones under the fine skirt. Shelagh was quiet, even more demure than Jane, and yet there was an occasional darting power in her that hinted to him of passion.

So again the businessman took breath, as it were, and skulked down to that dim-lit world of predator and prey. Again, in a white gleam centred in her greyish eyes, he saw her knowledge. He followed her. She seemed to know each wicket along the way; that he would make her pass him in the narrow hallway, breathing in; that he would have her strain forward to reach a tray, rather than pass it to her, so that her arms and chest must nearly brush him. But nothing happened: Shelagh was wise and dainty, with the self-preservation of the doe.

And what was he, the businessman, then? He liked to think he was the killing panther. He saw he'd been too careful, too polite to his women. Ceasing to scruple in his lust which was now terrible, he re-entered his own world of direct action. He decided his official relationship to Shelagh was no impediment since this business was his life and the restaurant his world. He stopped Shelagh as she moved off by herself to rest in the three o'clock lull between the lunchers and the drinkers. He asked her if he could drive her home when she went off work, or, if she wasn't too tired, buy her a drink. He saw that it was the right thing to do; Shelagh was unprepared and assented.

Out of uniform and in the basement bar down the street from the restaurant, Shelagh was less beautiful. She sat quietly, waiting. He wondered if she imagined he had a purpose on this occasion — for example, to fire her. He wished to behave *personally*, to resurrect his bachelor's charm from under the discreet despotism of the proprietor. He ordered drinks and leaned toward Shelagh. What to discuss? What else do you do with your time, Shelagh (had he already asked this?) . . . Have a boyfriend? . . . A beautiful girl like you, and so on until, Shall we go?

In the taxi he laid his hand along her leg, curiously pressing down with his thumb to feel the wary ligament he'd seen so often in his mind. She looked out the window. He drew the hand down to her knee. Are you going to ask me in? He felt that his desire was so strong that it stood up between them, that she must acknowledge it.

Would you like to come in? The game seemed to have gone out of her. Was it to be so easy? He expanded, relaxed, and his nervous lust bloomed out to full, easy assurance. He felt fondly toward this beautiful woman whose role he had created.

In the small beige and bamboo interior of her apartment she went off to change. He seated himself on a canvas chair, eyeing the dining room cup boards. He needed a drink. He waited. In a few minutes she came back wearing a wrap of soft denim which was attractive but somehow too functional, a garment to be by herself in. She sat across from him, distinctly tired, and put her knees together.

She poured him a drink and endured his presence while he drank it. With her arms around her knees, she was waiting for his announcement. Again the businessman felt encased in his role as boss, by her stubbornness. To seduce her would require much dexterity, much delicacy. She was not making it easy. She remained still when he came to sit beside her; she tolerated his humid breath around her neck. His desire was faltering until he imagined her in the flickering shade of his glossy restaurant. He saw himself reflected there; he thought of pressing her to one of the stuffed couches, his hands tearing the grey silk from her breast. He would be violent.

And then, on the very edge of force, he removed his weight from her. She adjusted her denim. It had been a mere point of pride that had stopped him, a quiet voice, a small check. But it had stopped him. He excused himself and shut the door behind him.

It was not difficult for him the forget that the evening with Shelagh had ever occurred when he returned to the restaurant. The fine-tuned eroticism of the decor became mere backdrop again, and the miraculous mushrooming of desire was gone without conscience. It simply vanished, leaving him pure and effective. Only once or twice when a curved body moved past him in the dark hallway did he recall the lust that had come leafy but without flower, there and in the locked rooms where he dreamed.

Is it necessary to describe how it was that each woman in turn after Jane and Shelagh roused him? How he saw in each a beauty and docility which fired him, and the servitude that turned his lust to arrogance? Without memory or imagination to track his path or project it, the businessman followed the peacock's feather over the months that followed. One, then another, of his waitresses inflamed him; each one was first wary and then unyielding; each dismissed him. He did not know he was dismissed. He only knew that at some juncture he did not persist. He wouldn't take it by force; it should have been his.

Until he'd been proprietor for a year. Two waitresses had left; he hadn't replaced them. He saw Cliff and the four other women moving around him like dancers in a galliard and realized how much they knew. They'd prepared each other and aided each other in resisting him. They'd generated a cool independence where their beauty was a harmony, a sunny plateau where he was not admitted. He grasped, by hearing a chance promise, that they even saw each other outside of work. He felt himself draw nearer to Cliff. He found himself admiring the man's ways with the women, envying the easy jokes amongst them which earlier he'd found somewhat obscene.

He vacillated between contentment and utter panic. He was accustomed to the decline of lust, but not to its burial, not to this preference he felt for its absence. He grew bitchy. He was annoyed by everything about the women. He wanted to become one of them and to destroy them from within.

Cliff tried to quell the businessman's tempers, but the

boss turned violently on his head waiter, calling him a queer, a castrated failure, a eunuch. He called him everything he could think of: he didn't know he had such thoughts. He ranted. He was irrational. Cliff stood with his lips pressed tight.

After the scene the businessman left the restaurant, expecting that his entire staff would walk out behind him and close the place down. He stayed home, wildly irresponsible, for the next day was a Friday and busy, long enough to control his shakes and shudders. He returned Saturday morning.

The sunlight lay on the leaves of the tropical birch. It ran lightly along the clay-coloured tiles. The mirror gave back bronze light to the walls. One could almost hear the birds at the tops of the leafy screens. At first he thought no one was there, but he saw Jane and then Shelagh, lovely shapes discreet and indiscernible as waterfowl going about their mysterious business. And Cliff, yes, even Cliff was there looking over the reservation book in the hallway. They were happy, peaceful. The businessman wanted to run like a wild boy among the tables, breaking tree-trunks and smashing chairs, turning the planters upside down and taking wrought iron umbrella stands to the mirrors, splintering the smoothness into hideous, jagged ends like the inside of himself.

But he was a practical man and he didn't want to destroy something which was his.

He walked away and never came back. He found a buyer easily; the staff was excellent and wanted to stay.

The Dragon

The Dragon

Pamela, they were saying, was one of those women who attracted violence. While he was simply a man who wanted to help people.

As a child, he did not understand the world. All around himself he saw people trying to escape their pain and calling it the pursuit of happiness. At seventeen he entered a seminary to train as a priest: at eighteen he met a woman and lost his calling. But she rejected him, cruelly. Having lost faith in God and woman simultaneously, he entered medical school. He studied hard and made his way to a big hospital in New York as a resident in psychiatry. He embraced certain theories and battled others, emerging despite it all with an intact belief in the possibility of human compassion.

He came home and set up office in a new, half-empty highrise in the centre of Toronto, the tracks of commerce shunting twelve stories beneath him. The walls were eggshell, the curtains unbleached jute. Light came from frosted tubes running in trenches around the periphery of the ceiling. The rug was the colour of damp sand. In the centre of the room was arranged an unstated circle: a chair with a chiselled heavy base, shallow swivel seat, and upright back and a matching but smaller chair opposite. Between the two was a table with an ashtray, although the psychiatrist, for that is how he had begun to see himself, as a psychiatrist, did not smoke himself. Apart from the digital clock discreetly placed, there was nothing else in the room.

The psychiatrist practised sitting in his chair and looking at the chair opposite. He swivelled around to look through his windows to the towers that were his neighbours. Beneath him were the faint rumblings of the fire-breathing city; up here there was only silence, austerity, and the moods of the sun.

Of necessity he became businesslike. He enlisted an answering service. He had bills printed on white sheets of paper, his name in light italic at the top. He began to get referrals from physicians and clinics: people began to petition him through his answering service. Please call, the messages said, urgent. The telephone answerer spelled out the names to him — Mrs. Horgan, Theodore First, Germaine Wilson — and repeated their telephone numbers. Calling, he discovered the numbers to be the city's government offices, department stores, and public schools. Need for him had sprung up just like that, full-blown, from the troubled brow of the city.

So it began. He opened his door to a patient. He took up his seat across the room from another human being less learned in the vagaries of the human psyche than himself, but no less sensitive, no less intelligent. His training let him ride his patients' aimless talk like a falcon, weightless, but with a claw of steel. He listened, mostly. He watched for clues — the twist of the mouth, the overflow of tear ducts. He did not wish to take notes while his patients poured forth their disappointments, so he grew adept at a kind of shadow filing, clearing out and aligning of information.

His patients' tales transported him. A man humiliating himself in ladies' clothing, a girl slashing her throat on her parents' bed, artists hacking their self-hate into icons, fathers crucifying their sons. And the women — he had thought he understood woman as he did man. But as he heard the virgin's terror of invasion, the matron's used emptiness, he did not want to learn what he was learning. He detached the names from the cases. He took cold showers in the mornings to forget his nightmares. At times he thought he suffered too much, but he persevered in his work. Sometimes he would come very near the heart of the other person; he could lean back in his chair and almost see the puffs of smoke separate from his body, in a kind of exorcism. Then he would deliver the standard apologia to the weeping person across the room: "I have done what I can for you. You know I cannot go out and slay the dragon."

So he learned to wear the hood of professionalism and live the role of the impersonal intimate. As he listened, his patients' neuroses bellied and broke. Sometimes there was healing. A few came to be free of their need for him, and more came to the door. The psychiatrist worked long hours. Sometimes at dusk when the last supplicant had departed, he would turn his chair to the window. The city smoke would fire the sunset to deep reds and burnished orange. Bewildered light would strike the curtains and lay itself on his pale walls. He'd see the tapestry of flesh and strife realized there, see a town lit by dragon breath and poised in positions of torture, the fat squashing the small, the weak scratching off the backs of the strong, as he sat cold-eyed in his swivel chair. What else there was of life for him — a renovated townhouse, dinners at good restaurants — continued somehow, tired as a vine wintering on rock.

It was in early September of his tenth year of practice that he received a request to see a new patient. While it would not be entirely true to say that his wan curiousity was quickened from the start by this man, because of what happened later the name William Kirk stood distinct when others disappeared.

A telephone message gave Mr. Kirk's business number, which proved to be the head office of a large advertising agency. The psychiatrist was put through several intermediaries before being allowed to speak to Mr. Kirk himself. When they were connected, the psychiatrist heard a sound like static electricity in the other man's voice, a sound of broadloom carpets and chrome bannisters. The man explained that he was plagued by certain worries and would like to speak to someone in the interest of preventing some later crisis. They arranged an appointment for Tuesday at 10:30.

Tuesday at 10:20 Mrs. Horgan left, her whorled peacock tail of guilt spread behind her, his pink tissues clutched in her soft fingers. The psychiatrist sighed. He had ten minutes to regenerate. Freud had prescribed classical music for the clinician between appointments, but he found music too stirring; most often he wanted only silence. He faced the window and waited. There was a soft click at the outside door, then an almost noiseless footfall on the carpet. From a corner of his eye the psychiatrist watched nine minutes pass on the digital clock. Then he opened the door and walked into the waiting room.

A thick-boned man whose wide still hands lay flat on his knees looked up at him. His broad forehead was slanted forward, his nose pinched, his eyes scooped deep, and his chin set as if by the grip of clenched fingers. He'd have looked surly if he had not been blond as a birch.

Kirk stood. They shook hands. The patient walked into the office behind the psychiatrist, choosing the correct chair without hesitation. He leaned back slightly. He lit a cigarette without asking. The two men eyed each other.

"Well, Mr. Kirk, what seems to be the difficulty?" The psychiatrist lowered his head and fastened a serene eye on Kirk's thick lids.

It was always difficult to name the problem. William Kirk, however, was more articulate than most. He had lost interest in his work and was unable to concentrate. He drank too much and couldn't seem to get a hold on himself. Oh yes, and he'd been divorced and now was involved with a woman named Pamela, who was an artist.

The psychiatrist found himself liking this man. He was more than a little relieved not to hear tales of motelroom whippings and the courting of small boys, for one thing. Kirk sounded gentle and intelligent. When the fifty minutes had elapsed, the two men shook hands again and the patient took himself to the door, opened it, and left the room. The door hissed along the carpet as it shut. The psychiatrist sat with his forefingers propped on the knob of his chin. Some of that love, that will to understand and make whole which he had once felt, stirred in him.

The second visit with Kirk was aimed at filling in the background. With a minimum of prodding, Kirk monologued in his modulated tones about an ambitious father, a pretty white house with hedges, and a mother who went to church. The psychiatrist was pleased. Kirk was a good storyteller; the professional was able to absorb the feelings almost as if it were his own small self pouring wine at the long dinner table, his own body drawn in the paternal embrace, with its smell of pipe tobacco and rough wool.

But when Kirk reached his adulthood and the woman who was to be become his wife, the psychiatrist asked him to stop. He didn't want to hear that yet. Instead he asked about the drinking.

Kirk grew excited. He spoke of alcohol as a beautiful destroyer, a she-devil. It makes me see heaven, he said, and drives me to a fury because it is all a lie. The psychiatrist said that alcohol was after all only an agent. And then, rashly disclosing something he barely knew he felt, said that he too had that anger, that wish to destroy. Where did it come from? At the question Kirk fell silent. When the session was over the two men parted awkwardly, as if they might have touched.

At their next meeting the psychiatrist hid his shyness in a stern, expectant look, and Kirk had difficulty speaking. He looked for long minutes at his fingernails with the day's dust under them. Then he said he had begun to realize how much was unknown in that room. He could create any self he wished for the psychiatrist: the other's vision was confined by the rigid corners of the office and took in no authority but Kirk's own. It therefore was beginning to seem impossible to Kirk that he would learn anything he did not already know. The psychiatrist suggested that he might realize that he knew more than he now was able to acknowledge. He did not say so, but he was hurt: he felt he had a lot to give to Kirk. They decided to try to increase the momentum of the therapy by meeting twice a week. They set the second hour for Friday at 5:30, the end of a long day and week for both of them.

The therapy did pick up intensity in the foggy ease of late afternoon. The psychiatrist settled in to listen like a needy child to a bedtime story, and Kirk spoke readily of how, when he was sixteen, his father had left the family to live with his mistress. He had come home from work at five o'clock, packed a bag, called Kirk's sister into the den to tell her, and then had gone away. From his bedroom upstairs, the boy had watched him drive off. He hated the mistress, although he never met her.

The psychiatrist remained wrapped in the story over the next weeks: the formal family meetings in hotel suites, the shrill voice of the mother alone at home; all of this seemed to sink into some empty place in him. (In his training he had long since worked through his own personal history.) For the first time he exceeded his schooled empathy. Moved nearly to tears by Kirk's first wounds inflicted by a woman, he linked his patient's prolonged virginity with his own celibacy. But again, when Kirk approached the story of his marriage, the psychiatrist made him stop. Claiming fatigue, he ended the session early.

When Kirk was gone, the psychiatrist sat alone, his hands pressed on his chest like bricks. He looked out the office window. It was evening, and the light drained off the city over the skyline, leaving only the glassy baubles that were the streetlights. The psychiatrist stood up stiffly, like a man tarred. Without knowing why, he moved around to the other side of the circle and lowered himself into Kirk's chair. He felt smaller. He saw a different vista. The sun had slid behind the bank tower, bronzing the windows along its path. It made a passage that seemed to stretch away from him, whitish and paved in glare, leading to some estate where he might have been welcome. That this path out was offered to the patient but not the practitioner seemed to him brutally unfair.

Clearly, by this time the psychiatrist's interest in Kirk had surpassed that allowed in the profession. The other patients were suffering from the inequity: the man who drank but was less poetic about it became a little boring; the woman who wanted more attention from her husband became petulant. Sitting there, the psychiatrist thought about William Kirk. He loved his patients gracefully, as the rescuer loves the victim. But with Kirk he had lost his distance. In his mind their two chairs had begun to spin around the circle, to spin and to blur like buckets on a wheel. He waited until the sun had gone down and then he told himself to go home and live his own life. The psychiatrist knew all about transferring love to a patient, and it was not the love which caused the scene in the end. The psychiatrist concealed his feelings.

The following Tuesday was the first day of winter. The sky was dark, and the wind was white. William Kirk arrived late and announced that he was reluctant to carry on the meetings. The psychiatrist was alarmed. He suggested that Kirk was resisting because they were nearing the most difficult, therefore the most significant, parts of the process; this resistance was nothing more than a fear that he, the professional, could not deal with the patient's darkest secrets. He assured Kirk that this was not so: he welcomed further intimacy. Kirk dropped his chin toward his chest. Tears stood over the depths of his pale eyes. They would carry on. The psychiatrist had won.

With that, they were in dangerous territory. Kirk spoke of his wife, a strong woman who had nevertheless fallen into step behind her husband like an oriental concubine. Kirk saw her draw her hair back behind her ears and become lifeless. She grew thin, her breasts drooped, and he stopped loving her. When their daughter was born, Kirk felt disappointed and excluded. Why? interjected the psychiatrist. Kirk thought that it was because the baby daughter seemed strange, foreign. A son he would have known as another like himself. But a girl — the baby frightened him. He had no idea what little girls were like.

"What are women like?" the psychiatrist asked softly across the circle.

And Kirk said, "I don't know. Women are mysterious."

"Yes," said the psychiatrist.

"The unknown," said Kirk.

"Quite," said the psychiatrist. He said nothing more, letting the words drain down to the carpet. He thought he had never known a woman. The young lady who had humiliated him passed through his mind. He had been seeking something unknown all these years; perhaps it dwelt where she was.

Then Kirk told how he'd left his wife, a story which shamed him, for afterwards she became so ill she was put in a convalescent home. The psychiatrist assured Kirk that the woman had found what she wanted. All that remained of the marriage was the daughter. The girl was no longer alien, but his, and Kirk felt that between himself and the girl there was perfect love. Of course, she was only eight years old. But the very existence of this love called into question his feelings for the woman Pamela: he could never love her that way.

It's not fair, said Pamela. She kept repeating that she'd never met the man. Perhaps she did something, said something to him. The violence seemed to have nothing to do with her. After it happened, she spent weeks powdering herself to cover the bruises and had to revamp her hairstyle because of the bald patches.

The psychiatrist and Kirk had suddenly arrived at the crux of the problem and almost as quickly at the solution. Kirk had never admitted before that it was the way Pamela made him feel that had brought him into therapy in the first place. She had been telling a story to her co-workers at the art gallery when Kirk had first seen her. He wanted to speak to her. Refusing to be interruped by his awkward presence, she continued the anecdote in a delivery punctuated with trills and gutter sounds, accompanied by waving arms. But he waited, and by the time the story ended, Kirk was in love. He pursued her; she gave resistance, but in time he won and was drawn into Pamela's crazy-wheeling life.

Pamela was dark-haired, gypsyish, he said. She looked thin as sticks in her dresses, but she was soft and white, like a cloud, in his bed. The first night Kirk slept with her she'd begun to bleed before dawn; her blood had streaked their bodies.

Night after night they spent together. They were in love. The only trouble was, said Kirk, that Pamela was a bitch. She had a very sharp tongue. The more he loved her, the more they fought. They argued about sex and food and light fixtures. Anything set them off, and each fight was more passionate. Pamela's words blinded and mocked him. Her little nails tore his flesh. Kirk felt himself turning inside out. He was like a bear, wanting to maul and crush. Pamela's small body simply went supple in his grip. He was forced, he said, to actual blows. Here he knew his advantage. He did not want to hurt her, but it was a battle with himself for control. He thought sometime he might kill her, by mistake. And there in the sand-carpeted office right in front of the psychiatrist, the favorite patient put his forehead in his hands and wept.

The psychiatrist panicked. He could not bear to hear this from Kirk, although, as always, the other man's experience was validated in his own body. At this moment when it was so important that he say something, he knew only his own forbidden feelings.

He let his mind lift from the room. That day driving to work he'd seen a whirlwind, a small, dark, city whirlwind, a thing that had no substance except for what it caught in its path. Dead leaves, tin foil from cigarette packs, and balls of dry grass were lifted into it. It was cone-shaped, condensed, a world in itself. It spun on the sidewalk. He remembered that he sat at the steering wheel without moving when the thing passed in front of him. Only when it was gone did he drive on.

It seemed to the psychiatrist then that the whirlwind had come into the room. It spun up and around the circle between himself and Kirk, taking the form of a bottle, of a woman, of himself. But the psychiatrist knew a hallucination when he saw one, and this he shook from his head impatiently. It seemed then to go right into his body. His heart pounded, and he was furious at the woman, the dragon, the way his perfect love had failed. And he knew that he could go no further: the treatment was ended.

You have gained considerable insight here, said the psychiatrist, and this itself can be a control on your actions. This is as far as I can go. And as an afterthought, as usual, he added that he could not, indeed, no one could, go out and slay the dragon.

In turn, Kirk said he felt remarkably eased by his admission. The fear seemed to have passed out of him. He would control himself. Perhaps he would continue with Pamela in peace, perhaps he would not see her any more. He felt cured.

Then they stood and clasped right hands, and William Kirk walked out of the office for the last time, the eye of the psychiatrist following him, glittering like an old stone.

He kept himself in a tight rein after that. He filled the empty spot in his timetable; he said the same things again and again to patients, sometimes with failure, sometimes with success. The city rumbled on below; the sun bled into the skyline. A year went by.

One Friday evening, the psychiatrist sat in his swivel chair after his last consultation. It was already dark, for winter brought down the night so early that people had to visit their therapists by streetlight. He had been working very hard. An invitation to a Christmas cocktail party lay in his briefcase. Looking down from his window to where the lights of cars drew their lines along the streets, the psychiatrist felt moved by a whim. Light of foot for the first time in months, he took his boxy leather coat from its hanger in the waiting room, descended in the quilt-walled elevator to where his car was stowed, and became one of those he watched all day.

In the moonlight the shadows of stripped trees marbled the snow. Through the bay window he saw that the party was an elegant one. The people in their holiday armour dazzled him. His feet slipped on the swept flagstone steps. And then he was inside, standing in the draft of the doorway, not at all certain that anyone knew him. Wineglasses winked, chrome caps on the light fixtures caught the belled reflections of a hundred mouthing guests. A host appeared. He closed the door and took away the newcomer's coat. Given a glass, the psychiatrist wedged himself into the mass. Milling, as if a leader might be thrust up before them to draw them away. A gap opened ahead; he moved toward it. And then he saw William Kirk.

Their eyes met. Kirk's face, smooth and sculpted in this light, opened with a smile. When he came forward the psychiatrist had to change his drink to his left hand to shake. The grip of hands, palm to palm, knuckles protruding, was like the wild thump of a heart. Kirk said something in his ear, but it was too noisy in the room. The only word the psychiatrist heard was Pamela.

The woman with Kirk was small, agitated, and dark, her face shaded by a disarray of hair. Her dress was loosely draped from a yoke resting on her shoulders. At the base of her neck was a small purple half-moon. Her eyes were very black, and she seemed to emit a musk. The psychiatrist hated her. He felt a flash of heat under his skin, and a great peace came to him even as he leapt to attack.

Almost no-one remembered seeing it happen. Too soon, there was only the detritus, the farcical final poses. A woman's shoulder soaked in red wine. A glass, his glass, unbroken on the carpet. A livid Kirk, pacing. The psychiatrist, prone in a corner. Pamela, bloody and screaming, surrounded by women.

The psychiatrist had struck William a sound manly blow to the lower jaw, out of a kind of respect: he must dispense with him first. Then he was at Pamela, lunging forward like a bear, arms curved above her in a mock embrace. He stumbled, then heaved his weight upright. A fist came out, retreated. Finding her body too small to strike, he closed his hands on her hair. He pulled. Masses of it came out softly, like dry moss, from her white scalp. She did not fall. She stood, thick red threads appearing around her forehead and running down her temples. She was still standing, clutching the empty wineglass whose liquid was spreading through the satin of her skirt, when they dragged him away from her. There was silence for a moment, then she started crying, and everyone began to talk. By the next day it was all over town, and some said poor woman and some said poor man.

Eternal Snow

Eternal Snow

It was late afternoon when we arrived at the parking lot half way up the mountain. The gondola terminal rose out of the snow, a space station, bright orange and blue girders like mechanical arms reaching up through the slash where the trees had been. I stretched in the thin air.

"Last chance to change your mind."

My voice was loud and hollow. Bill said nothing, so I slammed the car door: beside me, several little balls of snow separated themselves from the overhanging lip and rolled down to the packed road bed, a miniature avalanche. It reminded me of how my stepfather Harvey used to go shooting avalanches with the ski patrol. They'd ski across to the danger spots and then raise their guns, firing blanks, and the loud retorts would bring down perhaps a ton of snow.

"The snow looks great," I added.

"There's enough of it."

Bill had never been there before.

We lifted our suitcases and our skis out of the trunk of the car. I shouldered my skis the way I'd been taught to when I was six. This year I had fancy new bindings with brakes; they dug in behind my collar-bone and hurt. But I picked up the suitcase in the other hand. Bill had his skis and the Adidas bag we'd filled with liquor for our week at the top of the mountain.

It was beginning to snow thickly, in tiny dry flakes. The man who sold us our tickets for the gondola said that it had come down like this every night for a week.

On the platform we watched gleaming egg-shaped capsules swing down from the slope and into the terminal, caught in their bobbing by boys in orange parkas, who walked them to a stop. People who worked at ski resorts always looked the same: ruddy faces, bleached-out hair, the genial, bland expressions of beach bums. I'd known kids from high school in Calgary who'd turned out like that: they went to live in Banff and took jobs as chambermaids or tow attendants just so they could have free skiing on their off hours. They'd be nearly thirty now. I wondered what became of old ski bums.

It used to be that you parked your car here and rode the next few miles in an old glass-topped tourist bus. The bus drivers spoke to one another over a crackling radio. "Fifty-seven at number six, coming around." The turns in the road were numbered. Sometimes you had to pull over and let another bus pass, going the other way. Back then, Sunshine was a private domain for the hardy mountaineers in leather boots and woollen pants which bloused at the ankle. The change had been gradual: metal skis, buckle boots, more cars, a day lodge, and then the hotel. This Swiss gondola was the latest, new this year. It was supposed to be the longest in North America, with four separate cables and two mid-stations along its course. It brought all these spacemen in their padded jumpsuits and their moulded plastic boots which looked like they were filled with lead to help the wearers cope with zero gravity.

The orange-parka boy gestured us to a cab and held the outside rail to steady it as we stepped in. The doors shut with an electric clap. It was meant to seat six, but we were alone inside: only hotel guests went up at this hour of the day. We sat on opposite sides and stretched our feet into the centre to touch. I wanted Bill to know all of what I was thinking, to see how this place had been in the past. But he came from the east where I lived now, and he couldn't help but be a tourist, like the Japanese, the Americans. I felt the huge inertia of my unspoken emotions, a swelling resentment. I hadn't told him much. I wanted him to just know. It seemed to me that once no words had been needed. I had an image of being beside a man and having perfect, unspoken understanding.

The boy let go of the gondola and we jolted ahead. Looking out the plastic window I saw briefly the brown edges of old snow around the cuts for the road. Then we lifted high over the gulches and the spindly tops of half-buried trees. The ones with narrow forked tips we'd called "spinsters."

The white surface was forty feet below us: the snow cover, who knew how deep, over the ground. All you could see was white. I could tell Bill was disappointed in the view. I was too. I had liked it better from the road. I remembered looking out the window of the bus. I would have been eight or nine and Harvey was sitting beside me. "Is that eternal snow?" I had asked him, repeating a phrase from my geography book. Eternal snow lasted through all seasons: it never melted. I knew he would be pleased that I had heard of it. He gave me a quick look but didn't acknowledge — he never had — my cleverness. He looked straight ahead. "Not here," he said, "but a little further up."

Our room was smaller than I had imagined. Bill took one look at the little window, the double bed pushed into an alcove, and the single chair beside it and suggested that we go to the lounge for a drink. The lounge was called the Chimney Corner. It was dominated by a two-storey stone fireplace. A three-piece rock group was playing "American Pie". "*Bye*, bye Miss American Pie, Drove my Chevie to the levy but the levy was dry . . ." Around the tables sat the skiers, with their boots yawning open, buckles clacking. The day was over; these were the overnight guests, staying for the week as we were.

Firelight reflected triangles of red cheeks, thick necks, everywhere the arrow-head shape of bodies bulging out of unzippered jackets, turtlenecks. I wondered if Bill realized what it was to come to a chalet at 10,000 feet on a snow-driven pile of rocks in March with only a gondola that stopped at 6:00 P.M. for escape. When the light went off the mountain, there would be no place to come but here. These people would be our companions.

The roomful of faces was like an abstract painting. I saw the colours, the metallic lines, human shapes broken into bits. I knew it would change by the end of the week; it would be as if I had stood in the museum long enough to know the hidden objects in the work — lunchbox pear, table leg, glove. I would recognize every face and know the person it presented, at least I would know that facet of a person that he chose to be during a week's holiday with strangers.

But now we knew no one. We found a seat as near the fire as possible and ordered Bloody Caesars — in honour of the west. We held hands across the table. I looked outside. The tow had closed now, and the last skiers straggled up the slope to the lodge. Directly below us there used to be a small log cottage called Snowflake. We stayed there as a family in the fifties. When my father was alive, my mother used to go skiing with us. I was too young to remember much, but when I think back, I see myself walking out the door of that cottage, the snow on either side of the path as high as my parents' heads. After my father died and my mother married Harvey, only he and I went skiing. I think I loved Harvey more than my mother did. Often at Sunshine we would meet a woman who worked in Harvey's office. I would see her standing in the lift line and pretend that I didn't. "Oh look," Harvey would say in a tone of false surprise, "there's Miss Corbett."

The music stopped, and a tall dark woman in a green sweater, her matching jacket hanging from a crooked finger, walked into the lounge. Everyone looked at her, not only because she timed her entrance so well, but because she was over six feet tall and her black hair hung down to the middle of her shoulder blades. She walked between the tables and found a seat right in front of the fire, a single seat. The back of her head was between Bill and me. Her hair was so shiny it was blue, like steel. She ordered a drink, and within minutes a man was leaning over to speak to her. She answered him but kept staring into the fire. Then another man came and tried.

"You know what she is?" Bill whispered.

"What?"

"A skiing prostitute."

"You're not serious."

"Sure. They'd have to have them, in a place like this. You get your wealthy businessmen up here, they want something to do for the night. You can't get down the mountain, so . . . The management would know that she was here, they'd probably even give her special rates. She'd have just come one weekend and decided to stay. High-class prostitute. You can tell by the clean hair. Men like these would be worried about disease. The clean hair would reassure them."

Snow, when you poke a hole down six inches with your ski pole, is blue. Harvey used to say it reflected the sky, but I've noticed it's blue even when there are clouds. The sun did not shine that week, but the fresh snow kept coming, covering the hills every night with powder. The experts were ecstatic: in the morning you could ski over great trackless fields that swallowed your skis whole and let you skim like a bird over water, throwing up a cockscomb of the fine white stuff. I had never been able to ski powder well, though. You have to forget about edging, holding back; you have to just let your skis lie flat, keep your weight low, and stay close to the fall line. It takes nerve. I remember following Harvey straight downhill in the deep powder: I got going too fast and couldn't turn so I opened my arms and skiied into a tree.

"Don't unweight," my instructor told me. "Just give in to it." He was a man of about fifty, with red hair and a grizzled face. He had a trucking business in Northern Manitoba, but he came here every year to teach skiing for six weeks. It was the only way he ever stayed married to his wife, or so he told me. He had a sign on his fanny pack that said "Skiers make better lovers."

Bill and I were in the same class. I had more experience but he had less fear; in the powder we both floundered and fell a lot. We tried hard for the first three days. We had a lot of scotch that night and became living proof that high altitude increases the effects of alcohol: more was the only solution to our hangovers. On the fourth we took up a wineskin of port. We tried a slope that was called the Great Divide. If you drew a line among the peaks following the height of land, you'd have found the Divide: on one side all the water flowed west to the Pacific and on the other it flowed east. The Great Divide coincided with the border here. We passed signs that said "Leaving Alberta, Welcome to Beautiful British Columbia!" and then two minutes later a sign that said "Welcome Back to Sunny Alberta!" Bill took pictures from our chair.

On the way down we stayed on the sides. In a sheltered place we propped up our skis and began to drink. We laughed and I started pushing him around. He's a lot bigger than I am; he pushed me back into the drifts so that I sunk past my waist and couldn't get up. I struggled out and into my skis, feeling very huffy, and we went down for lunch.

By then we knew a lot of the faces in the dining room. They belonged to lawyers and accountants and Canadian Tire dealers and their wives with four sons. The women had been librarians until their second child was born and now were so busy and so game that everyone marvelled. There was a bachelor stockbroker who touched up his skiing every summer in the Andes and a doctor alone with his two children, who said his wife didn't like to ski. He made me think of Harvey. Ronald was his name, and on the first day he developed a crush on me. He'd barge in on the lines to share a chairlift. Bill and I had thought it was funny.

"There's your beau."

"Who, Ronald? He's not. Look, he's dropped me."

It appeared to be true. Ronald, who'd gazed at me across the dining room, who'd come over with his sullen daughter to eat with Bill and me only the day before, was gracing the next table, rubbing elbows with the tall woman in green with the blue-black hair. Bill put his arm around me to draw me out of my bad humour.

"He still likes you. He's just trying to make you jealous."

I looked at Ronald's daughter. Once in Banff Harvey and I had gone for dinner with Miss Corbett from his office, and he had taken me back to the hotel room first. "I'll just see Miss Corbett home," he had said. I had lain in my bed waiting for him to come for an impossibly long time. We shared a room; that was the type of economy Harvey was given to, although he had no need. Finally I had fallen asleep. In the morning he'd been just the same as before. I couldn't see Ronald's daughter anywhere.

"I'm sick of skiing," I said.

"I think I might take a lesson in the powder."

"Good idea." I didn't want to take a lesson. I knew I couldn't give myself up to that edgeless snow. It was like asking me to jump out of an airplane. No thanks.

"Maybe I'll go down the gondola and see how Banff has changed."

He didn't react to the way I'd excluded him but, typically, turned to the bus schedule.

"Just make sure you get back before the gondola closes at six."

"I'll take a cab."

It was the first time we'd been apart all week. I wore my knee-high sheepskin boots and beige cords and felt all unfettered after the ski gear. I was happy, sinking back on the gondola seat alone. Bill didn't take to Sunshine well. I noticed there were things I didn't like about it now too, but I had my loyalties to the past, and I wanted him to feel the specialness of the place even if it was gone. Unfair, wasn't it?

I looked down at the chairlift as I passed over and saw my admirer, Ronald, waiting in the line with the tall dark-haired woman. She was leaning forward over her poles, sliding her long legs back and forth along the snow. Switch, switch, switch. "You know what men call legs like that?" Bill had said. "Skullcrushers." He liked to say these things and see the combined shock and glee on my face. I didn't want to believe half of it, but I loved hearing what men said among men, echoes of a forbidden world. Because of the legs, we had taken to calling the woman in green Miss Tongs.

Miss Tongs sat every night in front of the hearth. A stream of men approached her. First guests, then instructors, then the employees of the lodge. She spoke to them all. Sometimes she got up and left the room, apparently following one of them. She always came back alone. Maybe Bill was right about her. Probably she was just what Ronald needed, I thought furiously from my gondola, my gaiety dissolving. Ronald had no pride. I couldn't understand this lack of pride in men. My best friend once told me that she had gone to meet her father in a New York hotel and had caught him on the telephone summoning a prostitute. "They all do it," she said. Do they? In places like this? If Harvey did, what did that make me — a victim or an accomplice?

Banff had changed from a mountain village to a tourist town in the years since I spent summers and school holidays there. The buffalo paddock still stood and the carved wooden bear by the museum, but new motels and condominiums built of cedar lined Banff Avenue, and the old hotel where the bus station was had burnt and had a new front. The Banff Café was still there. I went in and had a bowl of chicken noodle soup because I was cold. Once I'd been sitting there with a friend and the waitress had brought me a milkshake which I hadn't ordered. She said it was a gift but wouldn't tell me which of the boys at the counter had sent it. Later my friend and I walked out on the street, and the telephone rang in the booth on the corner. I answered it: it was for me. The same boy. He was across the street and wanted to ask me for a date. Boys had always liked me, and I had never been sure why. Similarly, I didn't seem to know if I liked them or not.

I went to the Quest shop and bought some earrings just to remind myself that this was today, not ten years ago, to prove that I existed now. Then I got a cab back to the parking lot.

It was after five o'clock. Snow was falling. The light had grown extremely flat earlier, and already most of the skiers had given up. I was glad I'd arrived before six; you never knew if they might shut down the gondola early, and then I would have been stuck in Banff for the night. Lonely and tired of memories, I was anxious to see Bill all of a sudden.

I was the only person going up. Four gondolas stood in line and the cable wasn't running. I chose the front cab. I could hear the boys talking in the control box.

"Won't it? It did that last time. Just throw it harder. Harder."

The gondola jolted forward three feet and then stopped. My cab moved just beyond the edge of the platform: below me was the road past the brown snow. The car swung. I was still close enough to hear the voices.

"I don't know — sometimes it stops and sometimes it goes." One boy pulled on a lever while the other laughed and boxed at his back.

I turned away, and then I was off. It was cold already, and the early mountain darkness was coming fast. I was hoisted over the disused bus route and into miles of snow. At first there were faces in the descending cabs on my right, the last skiers going out. Then there was no one. I was the only living thing.

The mountain was completely silent except for the low running of the electric cable, a sound like the purr of a refrigerator. I had never been alone on a mountainside before. I almost cried, I was so impressed by the hugeness of the rock and the whiteness of the snow, the thick sky over it. Suddenly the gondola seemed right. This was the visit I wanted with my landscape. I knew that snow so well. Moving over top it all I felt I was being carried to something stupendous. Then the purr stopped. My gondola swung just a little and was still.

I dangled there. Moments passed, and a sense of abandonment dawned. I coached myself not to panic. In ski class, Ronald had told a story about a man left overnight on the chairlift at Mount Tremblant. We'd also heard about the daredevil who went over a cliff right here on Brewster Rock. When they found him, the largest piece of his boot was the size of a potato chip. Or so people said. Ski stories involved putting oneself in danger of death, flirting, skirting the uninhabitable areas of earth, surviving where you couldn't survive; that was the whole idea. I wiggled my toes. The sheepskin boots were good but the cord pants a disaster: I had no long johns on either. The cable stretched in front of me, motionless.

Perhaps the gondola had been shut down for the night. Perhaps the operators had forgotten I was on it: they'd looked pretty careless. I don't wear a watch, but I could feel time passing in my numbing toes, my stiffening fingers. My backside was turning to ice. The man on Mount Tremblant had lived, but it couldn't have been this cold.

When we used to ride up on the bus, we would get stuck. Sometimes we had to get out and push the vehicle out of the drifts at the side of the road. It would slant and heave, the skis stowed in racks along its sides clanging. But we always got out of the drift, we always arrived at the lodge safely. The gondola was different, massive, electronic, impervious to human intervention. Should I close or open the window? Perhaps I could force open those electrically sealed doors and jump. It looked to be about thirty feet down at this point. But I had no skis. What if the snow was bottomless? I might sink over my head and not be able to move.

In any case, I wouldn't know which way to go once I got off. I didn't remember now on which side of me the road lay. If I found it, I could simply walk uphill and know that I would eventually reach the lodge. But what if I couldn't find it? Or what if I jumped and hit a rock and broke a leg? I'd have to judge the odds. Stay in the gondola and freeze helplessly or jump and risk the other dangers on the chance of reaching warmth. I decided it was too early to make a decision. Hold on, I told myself, you'd really be mad if you jumped and then the gondola began to move.

The purr started suddenly and the gondola jerked ahead. I was relieved, but not fully. I had the feeling that I'd glimpsed the face of my death and that he was circling to return. I passed the first way station. There was an orange-parka boy in there, clapping his huge mitts together. He saluted me merrily in my freezing bubble. I did not open the window or speak. I did not try to get out.

When the gondola stopped a second time, I wondered why I had done that, why I had gone meekly past the person who might be my last possible rescuer. Perhaps I was already suffering from hypothermia and had lost my judgement. This time I was dangling near a support pole. I began to wonder if I could reach the pole by climbing over the top of the gondola, as I had seen people do in a James Bond movie. Then I could climb down the pole into the snow. But I felt so cold I didn't think I could grip the rails. I had let the moment pass. If I died, what would the story be? Harvey hated people who postponed decisions until it was too late to make one.

I fingered my small paper bag with silver earrings made by someone in the Queen Charlotte Islands. Perhaps instead it would become a story about a vain woman who lost herself for the sake of a trinket, a narcissistic version of "Gift of the Magi"? I had bought the earrings to show Bill that I was able to enjoy myself without him. I had known as I bought them that to him they would be a reproof. A lover's quarrel ends in freezing death.

Was it time to jump now? I was very cold. Once I had frozen my feet black while skiing with Harvey. He wouldn't listen when I had said I was cold. "Tough it out," he had said. In which way was I to tough it out? If I jumped and succeeded, I would be a heroine. If I jumped and failed a fool. If I waited and died, a helpless victim. If I waited and survived, merely another epic ski story.

At least I should have had the wineskin. And why not do exercises? I stamped my feet, and the gondola started.

I went up and up, the empty cars streaming past me on their way down. They looked almost like company now. When I passed the second station, I waved to the orange parka and again asked no questions. The gondola stopped two more times on the last leg of the journey. Each time was less frightening than the time before. My death began to lose credibility; the truth was, the danger now seemed like a fantasy.

When I reached the platform my feet were like cubes of wood, and I stumbled out of the cab. The orange parka asked me if I had a pleasant ride.

It was cocktail hour at the Chimney Corner. I could hear the rock group with its tired repertoire. ". . . drinkin' whiskey and rye, singin' this will be the day that I die." I giggled a little, passing the door. I saw all the faces, known quantities now — Ronald and Miss Tongs and my drunken instructor. It was only six o'clock, and although I had been in the gondola for almost an hour, it was not even late enough for Bill to be worried. I knocked on the door of the room, and he opened it. I walked two steps to the bed and fell. He was buoyant, reaching to pull off my boots.

"You won't believe," he said. "I went up the chair with Miss Tongs. She's not a hooker at all. She's an aeronautical engineer from Orlando, Florida and she's never been on skis before in her life. What's the matter? Wasn't Banff the same?"

I was so cold I couldn't undress myself. He rubbed my feet and ran a hot bath. He held me while I lowered myself by inches into the steaming water. I remember I hurt more as the warmth invaded each cell than I had when the cold took over.

Going to Europe

Going to Europe

Gemma and Suzanne are sitting in a café in Juan les Pins, about to order lunch. They wear white cotton tops over their bikinis; sand clings to their oiled skin. Their eyes are blocked by round dark lenses. The waiter, poised, affecting servitude, looks from one to the other thinking perhaps they are sisters. Certainly one is blonde and well-rounded and the other is thin with red hair. But under the glasses their smiles are identical — expectant, wide, somehow false. They are laughing a good deal.

The joke, which he does not understand, first because it is in English and second because it is about something that happened half a world away, has to do with how on Sundays Suzanne used to drag Gemma out of her bed in the sorority house and made her walk a mile through the snow for pancakes at Smitty's. What loons they were! They walked to class together, arranging complementary timetables, had lunch and then sat in the library side by side, all the time talking and giggling and comparing passionately.

Suzanne pulls off her glasses to wipe away the tears. Gemma does the same. As they look down at their menus, the thin white starbursts in the corners of their eyes tighten. Watching, the waiter realizes that they are not girls, but women over thirty, accustomed to eating in good restaurants.

"Mesdames?"

One might choose fish, soup, salade Niçoise, an omelette. Suzanne was not terribly hungry when she left the beach, but now she can feel that familiar empty space wanting to be filled. She is eating too much. It has to do with being with Gemma who is always starving and never eats.

"Everything looks so good," says Suzanne.

"I don't see anything I want," says Gemma. Then she launches into a discussion with the waiter. Could she have the omelette without sauce or the salmon cold? She wants allowances to be made for her finicky habits. Gemma learned to speak French very well when she lived in Europe. At last, she pronounces.

"Soupe aux champignons."

Suzanne simply smiles and points her finger to what she wants on the menu.

"Fet-tu-ci-ne Alfre-do," the waiter enunciates, as if teaching a child. "Merci, mesdames." He bows himself away.

"Why don't you speak it?" hisses Gemma. "You can."

"I can't."

"You could if you tried."

"Oh, I could, but . . ." Suzanne cannot explain that a bizarre fealty to her prairie origins makes her feel fraudulent in French.

"It's weird. People can tell you understand. When you don't speak, you're like a mask."

"When you do, you're like a stranger."

The wine comes. The women lean back and look around them. The restaurant is on a corner with a view of the promenade one way and of the park with its dark Mediterranean pines the other. They have taken shelter in the dim interior rather than sit on the sidewalk because they are exhausted from sun and wind. It is still one week before the season begins in the French Riviera, and it is the time of the mistral, the cold wind that stirs up the sand. Even now, beach boys strut with their windsurfers before fantastically slim young women who tan topless. Suzanne can't help but marvel at the curve of the beach, the perfection of the bodies. To be sure, next week everything will be more fashionable, but Suzanne doesn't care. To Gemma this is a sign of her friend's lack of discrimination. She has already told the waiter that they came early to avoid crowds.

Gemma picks at the acrylic fingernails she glues over her own because she can't stop biting. She polishes these false ones and then picks off the colour. It is the one failure in her makeover. A thin, knowing career woman with henna in her hair, she fidgets constantly like an anxious teenager. She can't sit still in my presence, Suzanne reflects. And then, laughing softly, Suzanne brings up another of Gemma's failures. She'd left university one course short of a degree.

"Remember when you told Professor Guy you didn't care about his course because you were only going to get married?" Marriage had been Gemma's first idea of escape. "And he kept wanting to meet your fiancé?"

"It got so bad I couldn't go back to his class," Gemma says, beginning to giggle. "I didn't want that dumb B.A.

anyway."

Suzanne puts her hand over her mouth; her whole body is shaking.

Gemma blinks the moisture up from her lower lashes to save her mascara. "Anyway, what did it matter? I left right away for Europe."

The sudden mention of Europe blots up the laughter. The trip has been a sore point between the women for a decade. With no marriage on the horizon, Gemma grew desperate to leave Calgary: they planned to travel together after graduation. Gemma enticed Suzanne with pictures of four-storey buildings with iron stairs to come away from the awful place where they had the misfortune to be born. "You only hate it here because you're unhappy," Suzanne had said, unleashing the truth as if it were harmless. In the end it was she, who didn't much care for her boyfriend, who got engaged, while Gemma, betrayed, went to Europe by herself.

The silence grows between the two women. They still have not learned to laugh about this one. But it did seem to be for the best. Gemma found herself in Europe. She gained weight; she grew bold enough to travel alone; she had lovers. She was living in a cave with some Greek shepherds when her mother went over and dragged her back, using Suzanne's wedding as an excuse. The bridesmaid's dress Suzanne had made for her didn't fit; it had been designed for a child, not this returned Jezebel. In the wedding pictures Gemma looked sad and relieved, like a pet recaptured after a wild run through a shop. The extra weight fell off in her first month back in Calgary. And because for some reason Gemma never went back to live abroad, the sophistication began to seem like posturing.

"I would have killed myself after your wedding," says

Gemma, picking up the lapsed conversation as if the connection — her betrayal by Suzanne — were too obvious to mention. "If only I had pills. Something that wouldn't hurt."

"It wouldn't have been worth it. Especially since the marriage didn't last." It is an attempt at a joke.

"But it wouldn't have had anything to do with you!" cries Gemma.

"Suicide, unless it's disguised, is generally meant to hurt someone," says Suzanne rather primly.

"The reason you think that is that you see yourself entirely in terms of who you're with."

Suzanne rolls her fettucine around her fork and shudders. Perhaps she was wrong in suggesting that this year she and Gemma finally make the trip together. She did it because, with the marriage over and a few subsequent lovers gone, her past was dissolving: her best friend was a link. Does that mean Gemma is right when she says I define myself as wife of— or friend of— Suzanne asks herself. Perhaps. But it is also true that Gemma's prided independence, her aggressive singlehood, was assumed by default.

"I want continuity," says Suzanne. "I like to be with someone I love."

"I'm a lot stronger than I used to be," says Gemma. "I can honestly say I don't need love. I hate my father . . ."

"You're closer to your mother, aren't you?"

"Oh, I hate my mother," Gemma adds emphatically. "But at least if I killed myself, she'd understand it wasn't personal. Unlike you.

I give up, Suzanne thinks. It is just too complicated. They have moved to a table in the sun for coffee. The wind is still irritating. She scans the park, noting that the trees barely move because they are clipped short like show dogs. At home you can tell which way the wind blows by looking at a tree.

"Oh to live in the south of France," says Gemma. "I should be rich."

"Sidewalk espresso makes you philosophical." A peace offering.

But Gemma draws up. "It makes you look down your nose at me. Of course, you always did."

"I came with you, didn't I? Face it, in the end I never let you down."

Gemma lowers her head so her expression can't be seen.

The trip began in London two weeks ago. There, they argued about Margaret Thatcher's immigration policies — Gemma approved and Suzanne didn't. Suzanne thought *Ain't Misbehavin'* was superficial, and Gemma loved it. Cornwall brought no reprieve: Gemma called it "twee." Paris was next; among the French they nearly stopped speaking over the subject of extra-marital affairs. Gemma swore that she was more the victim of her affairs than anyone else. "In the end," she said, "the wives always win. Wives should be grateful; the things I teach their husbands must do wonders for their sex lives."

What do you know about wives? Suzanne wanted to scream. At least I *was* one. It was then she realized how Gemma had changed. Adventures in Europe and a decade of being single wiped out all they shared — the first rented rooms, the Delta Gamma pledge, the ski holidays. They had no safe conversation, and there were still two weeks to go. It seemed easiest to head for a good beach where they could absorb sun and wine and avoid dissent. And here they were.

It isn't going to work, Suzanne thinks, fingering her neck in silence. She can feel her skin tightening from exposure.

"I'm really the type to be rich," Gemma persists. "You know that's why I broke up with Rick." Gemma has often said that Rick was the only man who ever loved her. "I could see he wasn't going to make a success of himself. I could never respect a man who didn't make a lot of money." She taps a thin foot across her shin. "Poor Rick completely fell to pieces. He was crying in the corner."

"I guess that kind of behavior makes you feel contemptuous," says Suzanne. She is trying to commiserate: it is the best she can do.

"Oh no," says Gemma. "It would make you feel contemptuous, not me."

When they leave the restaurant Suzanne is uncomfortably full, and Gemma, who has only touched her soup, is still starving. Stopping beside the park at a man with a cart, she buys a Belgian waffle and devours it. She stands for a minute absorbed in licking the white sugar powder from each finger, then reapplies her lipstick. The friends agree to part for the afternoon. Suzanne goes back to the hotel, takes her book, and retires to the courtyard. She arranges her legs over the back of one of the wrought-iron chairs and moves her head out of range of a flowering cactus. Conscious of the fat Monsieur who runs the hotel eyeing her through the window, she holds up the book to hide her face.

What she does not understand is how she could have known Gemma all this time and not have seen all this selfish petulance, these cockeyed ideas. It is also a mystery how Gemma picked up her view of Suzanne. "It would make you feel contemptuous. . ." if a lover cried? Surely not. Granted, the early twenties were callous years, but was she so harsh, so brutal? And the business about Europe! Was it necessary to pay for that still? It was not Suzanne's fault that by the time Gemma returned all the right men were taken. It was not Suzanne's fault either that, after Europe, Gemma got herself a reputation. "I'm ahead of my time," Gemma would explain. Maybe she was. The trouble was that men — and Suzanne — operated from other standards.

What then did the friends have in common, aside from the fact that they had spent practically every waking hour together for four years? They met outside the Dean's office. Both had been rejected by their computer-selected roommates — Suzanne for having too many telephone calls and Gemma for playing her Association record too loudly. They sized each other up immediately as their only possible rival, moved in together, and began to borrow from each other's extensive wardrobes. They scoffed when boys asked out Gemma and then Suzanne, or Suzanne and then Gemma; the idea that a mere date could come between them was ridiculous. But just in case, they made a pact. They would never go out with each other's men — before, during or after one had staked a claim.

It was an easy bargain for Suzanne. Gemma had awful taste in men. She went for hockey players and dental students who took her to beer bashes and turned out to be married back in Leduc. But since she looked at men as opportunities to get something, no encounter was a loss; it all totalled that experience which was going to free her from her despised surroundings. With Suzanne the nice, desirable men — the med students and lifeguards — hung around endlessly, wanting to take her to meet their mothers.

Thinking about all this, Suzanne begins to feel uneasy. There is something she has always held back from Gemma. She remembers one day in spring when they were riding the number three bus back over the bridge toward campus. Suzanne announced her intention to save herself for true love. Not for marriage, she was smarter than that, but at least for love. In fact, she was not exactly saving herself with her lifeguard, but she made sure no one heard about it.

"For love?" Gemma had said. "If you don't have experience you'll mistake it for love the first time some guy turns you on." Yes, and that is just how I want it, Suzanne had thought.

Suzanne has been in the courtyard for forty-five minutes when Gemma is back, pulling up a chair. She is feeling good; she has met a man. "I'm not going to introduce you," she taunts. "You'd tear him to shreds."

Normally Suzanne would shrug this off, but today she gets angry. "I don't do that kind of thing," she says. "I don't know where you get your crazy ideas . . ."

"I guess I can remember what you did to just about every guy I ever went out with." Gemma picks at her nails.

"Well some of them were pretty dumb."

"I liked them. Remember Nicholas?" She giggles. "You scared him half to death that night you surprised us in the bedroom."

Suzanne puts down her book with a bang. It is horrible, how detailed Gemma's memory is of this other Suzanne. "The room was mine too. I don't go around trying to scare people."

"You forget."

"You make things up."

"Anyway you wouldn't like this guy," Gemma says confidently.

Suzanne decides to go indoors; it is too windy out anyway. It's *you* who doesn't like people, she says silently to her friend. For instance, you don't even like me. And yet you're afraid to be alone for a minute. Look how you follow me.

In the room Gemma wrinkles her nose at Suzanne's bikini and towel which are flung on the bed. Gemma is neat in her habits: even her dirty laundry is folded and stored in plastic bags that come from dry cleaners. Taking turns in front of the mirror, they get ready to go out for a drink.

The wind has dropped as the sun goes down; as its reminder there is only the soft clacking of pine cones over their heads. In the park the local men are playing *boules*. Gemma and Suzanne stop to watch. Suzanne loves the hypnotic roll of the black ball, followed by the men's united cheer as it slows to a halt in the right spot. Their game stops for a moment, and the men grin suggestively over at Gemma and Suzanne. The leers are forthright, confident. Suzanne fervently wishes she and Gemma could flirt back like innocent young girls. How much more compromising it is to be women without mates, well-dressed and over thirty.

"They're wondering what we are," she says bleakly.

"Aren't you used to that?"

"But it only happens when I'm with you."

"Thanks," says Gemma.

The bar they choose is large and busy, with waiters doing a kind of rhumba between close tables at knee-level. Beside Gemma and Suzanne is a group of people joking loudly. A pale man with a long nose leans over Suzanne. She looks into her glass, pretending she doesn't know French.

"He says he's the bassoonist with the symphony, and he would like you to hear him play tonight."

"Tell him we're busy. What are we going to do?"

"I was thinking of the casino."

Suzanne does not fancy cruising the gaming tables with Gemma. She frowns. Having discovered he can communicate through Gemma, the bassoonist leans closer. "Your friend is beautiful," he murmurs in French. "Tell her I would like to buy her a drink. Tell her I am not married." Gemma does not offer the translation but becomes bad humoured. It is necessary to leave the bar.

When they are in the street again, Gemma recovers her aplomb. "I can't imagine what he saw in you," she comments. "Your purse doesn't even match your outfit."

Suzanne is startled. Things have been getting worse, but this brings them close to the bottom. She hasn't thought about matching her purse to her clothes in years. The idea makes her sad. As they walk slowly back toward their hotel for dinner, the streetlights come on. Behind boutique windows pale mannequins gesture archly. Suzanne becomes sadder. It is true, then, that she is the one who has betrayed their friendship. She is the one who has left behind such cares as matched accessories. Gemma wants to try on clothes, but Suzanne doesn't feel like making the effort. She tells Gemma she is tired and goes back to the room. She has been sleeping for over an hour when Gemma comes in rattling paper.

"Fifteen hundred francs worth of new clothes!"

"Are you going to wear something new to dinner?"

"No, I'll just leave them in the bag. They're not the kind of things I'll get much use of."

"Why did you buy them then?"

"They looked so good on me I couldn't resist."

This is an old trick. When Gemma is down, she boasts.

Suzanne tries again. "Put them on to show me at least."

"I don't feel like it. My hair isn't right today."

The punishment will be long, then.

At dinner, Madam brings a spare man to their table. His name is Martin, and he is a Dutchman who runs a florist shop in Germany. Suzanne sits with her head cocked as he and Gemma banter in French. This must be the man of whom Gemma spoke. Suzanne smiles, intent on being not-scary. He smiles back, a lean face, a long obtrusive chin.

The meal does not progress well. Gemma is famished but will not take Madam's tomato soup. She dislikes the wine and is horrified by the tripe. Martin watches as she takes her fork and pokes a piece of fish, crying out in a cracked little voice. He tells her that it is good. She sulks, shakes her head, and says, "No, no!"

"Don't try to force her." Suzanne forgets. He wouldn't speak her language.

"No, of course not." Martin answers in slow, correct English. How smooth he is! By this one remark, he becomes conspiratorial with Suzanne; the two of them share instantly the custody of a troublesome child.

"You know," says Martin to Gemma, "it is a very nice thing to be able to sit down to a table and share a meal with people. Can you not do that?"

"Not when the food's no good."

The plate of fish is taken away by a wounded Madam. Salad comes; the dressing displeases Gemma. Speaking to Suzanne about his travels with his bicycle strapped on his car, Martin watches sidelong. He begins to pick the food off Gemma's plate. First a little piece of green pepper. Gemma smiles. Then he reaches over with his fork and spears a tomato. His own salad is sitting in front of him, half eaten.

"Hey," says Gemma.

He puts his fork boldly into her bowl and roots around for a slice of avocado. If he had moved her plate away from her, she'd simply have sighed in relief, but he did not. It sat in front of her, hers, and he stole from it.

"Eat your own," says Gemma, in French.

"Of course," says Martin. "I didn't know you wanted yours."

"I don't want it," says Gemma. "You can't trick me."

Now Suzanne laughs, then Gemma. They are disarmed by his cleverness; this man who drives along the coast in his Fiat, stopping overnight and taking his bicycle out for day trips, this amphibian traveller whose face, like his body, is long and hard as if to minimize drag. Dessert is crème caramel, and Gemma decries it swiftly. As Martin discusses with Suzanne the West German fondness for flowers, especially tulips, Gemma mutilates the custard, growing frantic for attention. Then as they stand up to leave the dining room, Martin draws Gemma up beside him and consolingly kisses her cheek.

"You are awful, woman," he says.

"I know I am," Gemma responds. "But I'm irresistible."

After dinner the three of them sit in the lounge under the curious gaze of the fat Monsieur. Martin shows no surprise at all that he is sitting in the middle chair speaking French to Gemma out of the right side of his face and English to Suzanne out of the left. Slowly, Suzanne begins to feel at a disadvantage. She is growing too tired to decipher the French. She guesses that what is happening tonight gives the lie to those charmed years of girlish intimacy. It is a wonder the women decided to come to Europe together at all. Suzanne has been wanting to save her past, while

Gemma wants to show hers up.

Suzanne stands up suddenly, and Monsieur's hard eyes flick away like insects down the wall. She sees a map of the town on the side table and notices that the hall where the symphony orchestra is playing is not far away. She tells Gemma she is going and leaves. Alone, she has a moment of pure bitterness. Isn't her friend unfair, disloyal, cheap? But the music makes her spirits rise. The soloist is a young blind pianist whose posture over the keyboard is alert, devoted.

When she comes back, Gemma is in bed. All her clothes are hung up, her makeup jars in a straight line, and her thin body barely makes a bump under the bedclothes. The old loyalty, even pity surfaces. Suzanne can understand something about this neatness. It is this: Gemma is afraid to make an impression. Having removed all traces of where she comes from, she doesn't belong anywhere. She uses everything so carefully because she feels she has no right to be where she is.

"You awake?" Suzanne asks gently.

"How was it?"

"O.K."

"Did you meet the bassoon?"

"I didn't stay around."

"He'll be *crushed.*"

"What about Martin?"

"Oh, him," says Gemma.

It remains unclear whether Martin, thus dismissed, has been seduced, regardless.

In the morning it is pouring rain, and over breakfast Martin suggests they go for a drive in the hills. There seems nothing better to do. Gemma rides in the front seat with him.

Beyond the rim of the town the hills grow steep, and there are farmhouses in the creases, with closed gates. From her perch in the back seat of the little car, Suzanne peers intently at the scenery until she is released for lunch. Tension has grown palpable. Running through the streaming air to an inn, they find a table. After Martin has ordered their food, he gives up his patter and joins the silence, looking in amusement from one woman to the other. It is unbearable to Suzanne that he should know his power. After the waitress has written all over the paper table cloth and gone to get the wine, Suzanne erupts in rapid, angry words. The weather is impossible, the place is boring, their trip has become too long anyway, and she wants to go back to London. Gemma agrees: she will visit a friend in Geneva. Tomorrow they separate.

As they drive back to town the clouds begin to part, but it is too late. Suzanne feels herself nearly home already. After dinner she leaves Gemma and Martin with Monsieur, watching the Coupe du Monde. In the room she finds their duty-free Hennessey. She goes to Madam and, using her French, asks for a glass to take to the courtyard. There, feeling very independent, she pours herself a shot.

The sky is now a transparent blue-black, ruffled with cloud; it could be the surface of a lake and the moon a reflection of itself. The gravel has bits of twinkling crystal in it. The flowering cactus has closed up for the night, and beyond the hedge Suzanne can hear the occasional explosion of a motorcycle. Madam comes out with a candle, and then Suzanne is alone, the Hennessey bottle gleaming like a witty companion near the flame. She supposes that tonight Gemma will go to bed with Martin. Perhaps she is doing so right now, in their room. This waiting outside of doors while Gemma is with some man feels familiar; it feels like something she has been doing for years. But in fact —

she examines her memory — it has never happened before. What did happen? Tears burn the edges of Suzanne's eyelids. How can one redeem the past when it flits from painful glare to shadow to regions utterly opaque?

Martin appears in a blue jogging suit, not the clothes he wore at dinner. He has been upstairs and has changed.

"Your friend is misbehaving. I have sent her to her room."

Suzanne says nothing.

"Do you prefer to be alone?"

"*Quelquefois,*" she says. "Brandy?"

He sits. "No. I am about to do some exercise."

Suzanne ponders the fact that he speaks English so much better than she speaks French. It is a habit of Europeans to speak other people's languages. She supposes it has to do with their being so crowded together and to having conquered each other back and forth over the centuries. It gives them a chance to pretend they are someone else for a while. Gemma insists she developed her personality — this other one — while speaking French. It all seems to Suzanne to be vaguely immoral. Not to speak a foreign tongue, but to want to be someone else. To be a Dutchman who sells tulips in Germany and drives through France looking for American women. To be a single woman taking a holiday with a friend at an expensive resort across the sea from home. She looks over the candle at Martin. His eyes wink, like the glass in the bottle.

"Did you come here to ask for the room?" she says. "Because if you want it you'd better hurry. I can't sit out much longer."

"Of course I did not," he says, implacably courteous. "Gemma is already in bed."

So had they, or had they not? Suzanne must not care. She toasts Martin. "To your success."

"You are flying back to London out of Nice."

"Yes."

"I will drive you to the airport. I must pass by there. Tomorrow after breakfast I leave." He stands and puts his hand flat on the table. My offer.

"Thank you," says Suzanne. "It will save me a bus trip." She picks up the glass and the bottle and follows Martin through the door. As they pass the lounge the fat Monsieur looks up from his papers and permits himself a small, inward smirk. Now the cyclist will have the other American lady? Not under your roof, thinks Suzanne.

Gemma is not even pretending to sleep. She is waiting, staring straight at the ceiling. Her suitcase is packed; the bathroom is cleaned. She looks at the bottle.

Suzanne drops her purse on the chair on Gemma's side of the room and then kicks off her sandals noisily. She spreads her clothes around the room. In the bathroom she splashes water on her face.

"Did Martin come to find you?"

"He wanted a glass of brandy."

"He did not, he wanted you. I should have known."

"He was yours. You met him first. I didn't even like him. If he was after me it was nothing I did."

"Of course it was. It's because you're so cold. That's why men want you. You're aloof. You don't care."

"I don't care about strangers. I came here with you, this was our trip, remember?" She throws her hairbrush at the wall. Then she realizes she has fallen into Gemma's trap; she has become angry, abusive. She picks up her T-shirt and throws that too.

At breakfast Suzanne splits their bill down to the last franc, 425 each. The division is salutary, an end to the trip. They laugh because it is so much like what women do. ''Fair's fair,'' says Gemma, taking the last of the Hennessey. Gemma is at least direct. Suzanne wants, suddenly, to be forgiven for all her — she won't say failures — omissions.

''Gemma,'' she says, putting out her hand.

Martin appears. ''Your bag?'' he says to Suzanne.

Gemma looks at them both. ''Is he driving you? But the airport is the other way. He's driving me to the train.''

Suzanne feels the crackle of approaching fire. ''I'll take the bus,'' she says, backing off.

Gemma pouts.

''I'm going toward Nice,'' says the man.

''But you promised!'' Gemma wails.

Suzanne knows she has made a terrible mistake. She tries to signal Gemma, but Gemma is too far gone.

''You can't take Suzanne, she's not your type!''

''Look,'' says Suzanne, in clear English which Martin will be bound to understand, ''we don't need this guy's games. We can go together by taxi, first to the train station and then to the airport bus.''

Gemma says nothing. No one moves. Suzanne thanks Martin and turns away from him. He does not leave but sits down at his unused place at the table. He looks at the plate in surprise, as if a meal has just disappeared before his eyes. ''Well,'' he says. Then he finds his smile again and looks up. ''Gemma then? May I drive you?''

She hardly wavers at all. She is not even looking at Suzanne when she speaks. ''I got myself the ride,'' she says, ''and I guess I'll take it.''

The Best Dog

The Best Dog

It is cold in Ottawa, and snowing; the plows are out on the street below the window where Penny sits, wrapped in a faded patchwork quilt. In her hand she holds a photograph. On the floor below her is the envelope it came in; the stamps are huge, foreign. The photograph shows a man and a dog standing on a boulevard. The dog is held close to the man's knee by a short leather leash. Behind them are large walnut trees, a border of moulting rose bushes and a tall wrought iron fence, the kind built around the closed city parks of Europe.

The dog is black and thick in the body, perhaps a little fat. The man looks boyish, but he too verges on plumpness around the middle. His lips — Penny holds the photograph up very close to her face — are pursed but open, as if he were crooning. Penny is able to tell this fact because she took the photograph, and at the moment the shutter closed the man, whose name is Mikhail, was in fact singing a love song. The song was in English, incomprehensible to passers by but not to Penny, nor to the dog, who understands in English such simple words as dogs do understand.

The dog holds in his teeth a small black leather pouch. It is a matter of pride to both dog and master that the animal can be trusted to carry this pouch when the two are abroad in the streets. In the pouch are stored the man's identity papers, his money, and also the permit which allows him to take the dog on city buses. This permit, which Mikhail would gladly draw out to show, names the dog "Mike." The fact that the man and the dog have the same name is an accident. Mikhail received Mike through a friend at the American embassy where the dog had been abandoned by his previous owner, who had been on his way to Africa and had been advised he could not take a dog with him. Mikhail and Mike have been together for five years, and are so devoted that an engagement — Mikhail's third — was broken over the issue.

All of this, and more, Penny remembers as she looks at the photograph. Penny reaches to the floor and pulls the stamps off the envelope; her nephew collects. She holds them close to her face. Detailed as engravings, in faded turquoise and orange, they look like antiquities. She can hardly believe that this picture was taken only eight months ago and by her, for she really is in the picture, just a few feet away from Mikhail, behind the camera.

In London, she had sat in the Transit Lounge on a plastic chair, congratulating herself on being sent, with her minister, to Eastern Europe. In Zurich, drinking water that cost two dollars and fifty cents a glass, she watched for travellers going her way. They were mostly men in drab suits, representatives of British firms. Their conversation was about the long waits for service in these countries, the lack of night life, the dullness of the citizens. When the aircraft was ready to board they all had to go out on the tarmac and point to their luggage, stacked under the belly of the plane, before it would be loaded. Men in blue overalls closed the airplane door. When it was opened again, they had landed. Penny stepped out into humid, close air. They had been told that someone would be waiting for them.

"How do you do Mister Doctor Minister Kling. And Miss James. I am Oana, your translator."

The other passengers were loaded into a bus but Penny and Gerry, her boss, the translator and two men walked across the tarmac into the terminal building. The men made Penny nervous.

"You have been in our city once before," said Oana to Gerry, "but . . ." She turned her dark, unreflective eyes to Penny, "this is your first visit." These were not questions.

They waited in a private lounge while their visas were processed. "Exactly the same as last time," Gerry was saying in Penny's ear. "Right down to the plastic cover on the footstool." There were plum velvet sofas and padded chairs, but all were draped in dust covers. "I wonder if they take them off when the minister comes." Penny did not laugh but smiled brightly at Oana who stood a little to the side; although she did not appear to be listening she might have heard. Penny did not wish Oana to take offence.

"That's a standard sort of joke in our civil service," she thought of saying. "It says more about us than about you." But the smooth cheek, slightly hollow, and severe lip line did not encourage her, and she kept silence.

Half a dozen men loaded their bags into the back of a

black car. All the cars in sight were identical, small four-door sedans with tapered front and back. It was evening, and growing dark. There had been rain and now the streets were glistening; the cars darted off the arrivals ramp and into the traffic like drops of water down a window pane.

The streets were wide and the boulevards full of rose bushes. It was September; the petals were just beginning to fall. A group of women wearing wide skirts and kerchiefs, holding scythes, walked along the edge of the road. The gardening crew, going home for dinner.

The car turned into a traffic circle in front of a tall edifice with three towers.

"This is the Press Building. It is very much in the Russian style," said Oana. "Everyone knows about Russian architecture." She smiled over her shoulder from the front seat, wrinkling her nose: it smells. Gerry elbowed Penny. "They make anti-Russian remarks to gain your confidence," he had said. "Don't follow suit."

"Your English is very good," said Penny.

Oana turned to look at the road again.

"You've come in the best month. September is always fine. And there are some very nice events planned for you."

After that, silence as they drove along. The driver held the wheel with both hands, right at the top, and took the turns suddenly, on two wheels.

Mikhail looked more like a leading man than a hired guide; he was tall, black-haired and wore an expectant expression along with a red carnation.

"I had hoped it was you I was to meet," he said, bending to kiss her hand. When he stood up a pair of moss-soft brown eyes rose to hers. "But I was afraid to approach such a beautiful lady."

It was dinner time. The small black car waited in front of the hotel: Gerry and Penny and Oana and Mikhail were going for dinner. The driver stood beside the car door, holding it open. He wore dark blue coveralls like the baggage men in the airport, and had a long, turned-down nose. He was to be with Gerry and Penny for their entire visit. As the car whirled through the traffic circles he spoke loudly in his language, pointing out the museums, the communist party headquarters, the university. Oana translated. Mikhail, Gerry and Penny were shoulder to shoulder in the back seat, leaning first one way and then the other on turns.

In front of the restaurant the driver jumped out and opened all the doors. He stood back as Penny alighted and then stood forward to shut the door. In his baggy worksuit his decorous motions looked comic. As they walked away he watched.

"What's he going to do?" said Penny to Mikhail.

"Wait until we finish and drive you home."

Mikhail led the way through a frosted door. Inside, a series of rooms opened, like something done with mirrors. Waiters with their backs against the wall bowed; the chairs were velvet; rose-coloured lamps glowed from sconces. The maitre d' led the guests past a crescent-shaped table spread with game hens and pheasants and salmon, piles of cheeses and cakes.

In the pink light, Mikhail's black hair and pallid skin looked decadent. A pearl grey ascot stood at his neck. Penny remembered the feel of his palm when he had grasped her hand; hot, moist. Now he patted his brow with a handkerchief. For one so composed, he sweated rather a lot.

Mikhail ordered the meal; as Penny listened, the words began to have a shape to her. They were rather like jigsaw pieces, fitting together smoothly, but each having funny protuberances. "Would you like the fish or the stuffed pork?" he said to her in English. He had a cleft chin and those very frank, very brown eyes. She chose the fish.

Effortlessly, Mikhail made himself the centre of the conversation. He had three last names. Now he only used two; even that was too many for some people. It was too many for Oana, clearly, who had unfolded her napkin and was staring at it in disapproval. "I like to put the other on my card, to write it down," he said. "I wouldn't like to lose it, because it was given to my family by Napolean."

He spoke in a matter of fact tone. His grandmother had been a Russian princess; his father's name was one of the oldest in the country. These things, like the black caviar which arrived in a pot with lemons on the side, were messages he seemed confident they understood; he offered it all to make a contact that went beyond the present situation. He had been seven years old, he said, when things changed. That made him forty, now, Penny calculated, ten years older than she was, ten years older than he looked.

"My first pet was a pony," he was saying. "He was so devoted, he followed me everywhere, even in the house. When we lost everything, the pony was given to a circus. And he was so sad there, he refused all food, and he died." Mikhail picked up a triangle of toast, buttered it, and used it to scoop a great hunk of caviar. He squeezed lemon on the caviar. Then he put the whole thing in his mouth.

"Mikhail writes poetry," said Oana. "We both work with special visitors, sometimes together, more often not."

Mikhail appealed to Gerry. "I believe you must do something in this life, otherwise you are like an animal. You just get up, and eat, and do some work, and wash the dishes and go to sleep. I like to make something. I even think of putting some poems in a box and burying them in the ground."

Gerry nodded, looking uncomfortable.

"And you, what do you think?" said Mikhail, turning to Penny.

At that moment, Penny was thinking about the first thing he had said to her. ". . . such a beautiful woman . . ." It was not true. She was not beautiful. She had a long, luminous freckled face and looked sad. Sometimes men became interested but soon they drifted on. Accustomed to disappointment, she was happiest when she met someone new, and could work the temporary magic. She sipped her Reisling and instantly felt giddy.

"I am so interested in your country. Here, people are very serious."

Seriousness, Oana could speak to. Everyone worked so hard. Her daughter was training to be an electrical engineer; Oana helped by watching the baby nights. There were also meetings to attend, and the shopping to do. But Mikhail! He might work for ten days as a guide and then have a week free, to stay home in the apartment he shared with his mother and enjoy the nice things they still had: a collection of porcelain, a small gem collection. He spoke five languages, had two degrees.

"I am an elitist," he said. "For me, freedom is necessary. I know what to do with it. But most people here would not know. And so I can be rather happy. My dog makes me happiest of all. He is a purebred Labrador retriever. I put him in the shows, but he can not win the medals, even though he is the best. He has no pedigree, you see. His pedigree is in the United States, where he was born."

Oana made a noise between a cough and a snarl and

pointedly said nothing. Gerry dug into his stuffed pork and did not look up.

"Yes I really love my dog," said Mikhail. The way he said love, it sounded like "laaa-ve."

Penny felt she had travelled deep into a vault of history, and was witness to old splendours, old rivalries. The play of distaste between the two guides merely made the experience richer. But as they got up to leave the restaurant, the setting began to falter. Mikhail stood back while Gerry paid for the meal; his aspect — relaxed, confident of being looked after — made the dark man seem a flatterer, a paid companion. He suggested a bar. But outside the frosted door Gerry looked pointedly at the car. It had been much more money than he expected, and there had been a fuss about travellers' cheques.

"Where can we drop you, Mikhail?" he said.

Mikhail began to give the driver directions. The driver shook his head. He would not open the door.

"Tell him we are asking him to drive you home," said Penny.

Mikhail spoke again to the driver, who this time responded with a torrent of angry syllables. Mikhail shrugged.

"It will not be possible," he said. "This man says he works for you and not for me. It is not unusual," he said, and reached for Penny's hand, kissing it. He strode away quickly. Oana had been standing in the shadow by the door. Now she stepped forward. She announced that she would go home by herself, on the bus. At that moment it occurred to Penny that the translator had not been necessary that evening, since Mikhail spoke excellent English. Penny looked at Gerry for a signal. They had been warned about the KGB. Could it be true, they were being watched?

In the back seat, Gerry settled himself angrily, bracing an arm against the door for the hairpin turns. "Some kind of nut," he said, "loves his dog."

"I think it's a cultural difference."

"You ask me, he's trouble. Something strange about his relationship to the rest of these guys."

"He speaks so well."

"He must have something. To have wangled himself the kind of freedom he's got."

Penny was watching the back of the driver's neck. The hairs were bristling.

There was a lot of this blank-faced watching. In the hotel you might walk up a staircase from the lobby and see a young man in a neat suit sitting motionless on a chair. Four hours later, you passed again and he was still there, and he had been joined by another like himself. Dull-eyed, the two would share a cigarette.

There were also the uncompromising young women at the desk making tourist arrangements. They would tell you without looking at a list or picking up a telephone that there were no tickets left, no cars left, no messages, no telex, no airflight information. "They are there to help you," said Oana. "Believe me, it would be worse, otherwise."

The meetings took place over heavy luncheons which began with plum brandy and ended with vodka. A deputy minister had been replaced since the last mission; there would be several days' wait. Penny went out in the city. Mornings were hazy, that unreal golden light coming up slowly. She visited the open air market, and it was as if she were walking in a creche, a city of stage paste, so temporary did it feel.

Women in plastic sandals and ankle socks queued for a truck's arrival. Penny touched braids of garlic, poor apples, peppers and squash. She stopped before a gypsy woman selling bricks of something honey coloured. Was it candy? She raised some to her mouth as if to bite. "Nu, nu." The woman put her hand by her mouth and laughed, showing black, stumpy teeth. She picked up the brick herself and mimed smearing it over her legs. She said a word. Penny did not know what it meant. She looked at the brick again. Beeswax.

"Beeswax," she said, also laughing. "Depilation."

"Da!" said the woman.

"Ouch," said Penny. "No thanks."

The shops held little painted wooden objects, doilies with red embroidery, thousands of peasant blouses. Penny wandered all afternoon; some of the old buildings had huge cracks down their sides from an earthquake. She returned to the hotel in the still, leafy incandescence before dark. Mikhail was waiting by the door, wearing white jeans and a green satin jacket with a felt insignia. Now Penny noticed how different his clothing was from the clothing of his countrymen.

"Nice jacket," she said.

"A gift from a tourist," he said. "It's the uniform of the Swedish soccer team." He stepped away from the wall; he was leading the black dog.

"I wanted you to meet Mike."

Mike extended a paw. He was a large, thick-necked dog with an intelligent face. His sleek fatness reminded Penny of a seal, so short-haired that he seemed more than naturally naked. He sat, and made unavoidable the sight of his upturned genitalia. He preceded the trio in the walk to the hotel, his back legs stiff and slightly bowed, his hindquarters switching slowly first one way and then the other.

They took a table in the courtyard. The dog sat at Mikhail's knee and did not move when the waiter admired him. Mikhail had come to show Penny the route of a tour he would take her on, north to the mountains. Gerry would stay for more meetings. The guide leaned against Penny's elbow as he pointed to spots on the map. When he walked out with his dog, people stared.

But the next morning, Mikhail was alone, standing stiffly beside the driver in front of the hotel. On the road, peasants soon appeared, pulling wagons and leading cows on chains. The driver settled his eyes on the highway and Mikhail slid his arm silently along the top of the back seat, behind Penny's shoulders. It was frightening, thrilling, to be sitting that way behind the hostile driver. The heat of his body reached Penny; in front of her was the thick, close-shaven neck of the driver. The subterfuge was so complicated: Mikhail was guide, and guard. That he — they — were subject, watched, at the same time, seemed to add depth, like a dark line around their images.

They entered a narrow roadway blinkered with pine. The forest had once been filled with robbers, said Mikhail, and was burned to make the country safer. More trees were planted; now it was a park where families came to picnic and paddle boats. In the parking area Mikhail spoke to the driver, looking at his watch and indicating three hours. The driver said nothing. Penny was convinced he hated them both.

That day the boat which took tourists to the island was not operating. Mikhail walked up and down the shore, gesturing to the dock on the far shore, where the ubiquitous men in coveralls sat beside barrels, but the long wooden vessel stayed tucked down at the edge of the water. He went to the kitchen door of the inn to borrow a telephone. Penny stood along side smiling uneasily at a small woman with hands covered with warts, who was slicing bread.

"I think we will not get a boat today." Mikhail was irritated. "What do you think if we have lunch here?"

But the restaurant would not open for another hour. They walked on the edge of the lake. It was lined with reeds, and over the top of the water rode a blue mist. A boy was rowing a skiff amongst the rushes and the wisps of fog, pulling his craft back and forth crazily with just one oar.

"Here is the song I wrote for Mike. I have the words written down. He likes very much to hear me sing it."

"Sing it for me."

"No. But you can look at the words." He handed Penny a piece of onionskin, folded into a small square. She opened it.

Who comes to my bed each morning, eyes so bright
and smiling
whose tongue is warm and touches my arm,
who guides the door at night? It's Mike!"

Mikhail was walking very close to her, the weight of his body occasionally swinging against hers. Suddenly he turned to face her and took her face in his hands. His lips pressed on hers. There was so much force in the kiss that her teeth were bared, her lips pressed right back. When he pulled away she stood with her mouth open, a little noise escaping her.

"Why do you not look me in the eyes? Is it so dangerous?"

She decided he was a professional seducer. She was not sure, however, whether that was going to matter.

At the inn, he insisted that they have a table far along the porch, away from all the other diners. They ate sausages made by the monks at Sibiu and the white, tart cheese which came from goats. Water lapped at the wooden posts beneath them. The retreating feet of the waiter made hollow sounds on the floor. Sometimes, when travelling, which Penny had begun to do a lot in her work, she came to a place which fit instantly into her affections as if a spot had been made ready for it. She could not believe she would never visit this lakeside again, that she would not be able, much later, to set out through trees and find it.

"Here, at last, there is no one listening," said Mikhail. "Did you know there is always someone? The driver. Even in the park, there was someone watching us."

"Does the driver speak English?"

"It is not important. He is not a nice man, some are like that. But he is insignificant. Do your friends call you Penny?"

"Yes."

"That's too bad. You should have a longer name; that is a baby name."

Penny might have thought something of the sort herself, but she did not like to hear it.

"You have no rings on your left hand? You are not engaged?"

"No."

"I would like to call you Elena. It is the name of my first fiancée, Elena. She was very like you. With blonde hair."

"You only just met me."

"No, it's not true. I have met you many times before."

Penny grew stiff.

"Why do you pull away? Do not pull away from me." He put one hand out as if to strike her cheek; then he laid it softly against her head. "Look me in the eye."

She looked, with effort. Behind him she could see that the child in the skiff had appeared below the deck. He was banging his oar against the posts sunk into the water.

Bang, bang, bang.

"I am like a bird in a cage. And I have to sing that the cage is golden. We are so happy here. That is what I tell you. I tell all the tourists. I have seen people from almost every country. And I myself have never been outside. I am trapped here. Nobody can I trust. No countryman can I talk to. And so I fall in love with you, and you go away next week and I am more alone than ever."

The tears began to run down his cheeks. They were like tears running down the face on a billboard; they made no alteration in his voice or his posture.

He has said these things before to a hundred tourists with no rings on their left hand, Penny was sure. It was part of the tour, perhaps. But that did not make them any less true.

Penny and Mikhail were walking back through the replanted forest. They had gone the long way around to the parking lot, for the fun of it finding routes where it seemed no one could be watching. The spruce trees stood a hundred feet in the air on either side; the very lowest limbs swayed above their heads like dark, oiled fans; the bare earth was soft with needles. They were holding hands. Mikhail was singing the song for his dog. Penny committed to memory the exact angle of his chin as he lifted it to the sky on the refrain.

"Who guards the door at night? It's Mike!"

She joined it, it didn't matter what the words were. It was a silly song, that was all, silly for two adults in the service of their governments to be singing in the woods.

Mikhail led her to a bench by the path. He sat very close beside her and put his arms around her.

"What is it like where you live? Is there a lot of snow

there? Can I see through your eyes — is it bright, empty?" He kissed her again, hard. This time she was ready for it. She braced her neck against the pressure, kept her lips shut. In a second, he understood. She opened her eyes, but his were still closed. He was slow to let go — an idea, a possibility dropped.

Finally he sat back, away from her.

"There is something. Something that I wish to ask you."

The bench faced a straight line of trees, straight as the teeth in a comb. There was a man at the far end, walking across the clearing. When he had crossed, the vista opened, it seemed to stretch right to the airport, to the dead sleep across the Atlantic, to crisp, clean, red and white Canada.

"You are the only one who can help me."

The words fell on Penny like grace. No matter how many ladies he seduced, no matter how many men left her, she was, here, today, the only one who could help. What would be his pleasure? Her participation in a dangerous mission?

He reached into his back pocket and drew out an envelope.

"It is nothing illegal," said Mikhail carefully. "It is fine for you to do it, but not for me to do it. It is fine for you to do it for me. You must take this with you to Canada, put in the eleven dollars, and send it away for me."

She took the envelope. It was addressed to the American Kennel Club.

"When you receive the pedigree, send it to me here. You know it will mean a very great deal to both Mike and I. He can have his medals, which he deserves, to show his breeding." He said no more about love.

"By now you will have learned," Penny wrote, "that there

is no possibility of getting the pedigree for Mike, without the name of his dam and sire. Since you have not given it to me I presume you do not have that information."

Beside her was a pedigree, torn to pieces. Outside the snow was gathering more and more thickly; Ottawa winter was so long. She had written the Kennel Club and was unable to get the dog's papers. So she had gone to a friend and had a pedigree forged, easy enough to do when you know people. She had even got the thing ready to mail. It had been Gerry's idea, actually; he said it was a small thing to give the guy a charge. And it would give Mikhail a charge; Mike might officially become what his owner believed he was, the best dog in the country. Mikhail would have that to remember when faced with the likes of Oana, who had reported him for inappropriate behaviour with visitors, or the driver, who had, astonishingly, simply abandoned them that day in the park, leaving them to hitchhike.

But when she saw the photograph she knew she was wrong. She had taken the forged pedigree in her two hands and ripped it in pieces. Mikhail did not fall for false things. He knew caviar and Chinese porcelain, and he had trusted her to help him. "If there is anything else I can do, please write," she continued. She had no idea whether the letter would reach him.

Home for Good

Home for Good

When the affair broke off for good, Suzanne went back to Calgary to live. It was a transfer, in fact a promotion. Everyone in the city was rich. The skyline had sprung up like pistons and houses in the old neighbourhood were being bought up by millionaires. Only the river was the same. Lyall and Bonnie lived along it, their back yard rose from the shallow banks and spread up the hill between willow trees to the glass doors of the dining room. There were two cars in front and three children downstairs somewhere.

The broadloom looked like an extension of the lawn. It flowed silver green under Suzanne's feet and seemed to buzz with static. She sat listening to talk of the boys' tennis and a house boat in the Kootenays feeling that their childhood had been one long trick. Perhaps it had not happened with these people at all, perhaps not in this place. Memory, at any rate, provided no environment, and she had little to say to them.

As Suzanne stood to leave, she leaned over and poured the dregs of her tea into a plant pot. It was a habit she had from living alone; someone had told her once that cold tea was good for plants. Lyall jumped. His face crumpled oddly, like a ball with a puncture in it. "She's going to kill our plants," he complained to Bonnie. It was an awkward moment. He sounded like a fearful child who believed others had the power of life or death. He sounded as if he saw Suzanne as a stranger, a dangerous viper who could poison this, his carefully built refuge.

In a sulk, she went back to the apartment she had yet to furnish and headed straight for the kitchen sink. She was going to wash every one of her white dishes before she put them in the cupboards where they would stand in racks in order of size, irreproachable. She had come home for help, really, yet her reappearance seemed to be a threat. Thanks to their mothers, everyone knew about the married man. In this town, Suzanne was a marked woman, one who had ventured off the ordained path, a bad person, even. She banged the plates into the drainer. Lyall of all people ought to understand, being a bad boy himself.

She turned the hot water tap hotter. Just as she dipped her hands back into the painful, bubbling bath the telephone rang. She let it go four times, so that the caller would know it was an inconvenience, and then dried her hands and set out to find the phone. It was on the floor behind a crate of books.

"Hello mother."

Her mother called several times a day to find out how she was feeling. Someone who had been jilted by a married man may deserve what she got, but none the less a daughter's grief must not be ignored.

"I'd rather do it myself," Suzanne said, "honest, I know where I want the stuff to go."

At first Suzanne had resisted coming home. Finally it was a decision less to come here than to leave the other place. The job would be good, and being near her parents a comfort, she had supposed.

"No Mom, I haven't called Gemma."

She had no intention of calling Gemma. She was out of touch with nearly everyone. They had gone to school together, but in their twenties they had so energetically taken up the things called lifestyles. Great barriers had been raised by the kind of music one listened to, by how much money one had, or wanted to have, by whether one lived downtown or in a suburb. On visits home Suzanne had felt superior to her friends even though they had houses and cars and she lived on the third floor of what one of the few of them who travelled east had called a boarding house.

It wasn't a boarding house, it was a townhouse cut into apartments, and it was an apartment much envied by her Toronto friends. It galled Suzanne that her sophistication, her interesting job, the artists and homosexuals she knew only made the old crowd feel sorry for her. And it galled her more that their pity affected her, that she *minded* if in their eyes she was not making a success of her life.

But now they were over thirty and surely the self-consciousness had gone. Moving home, living here had put Suzanne in a sentimental frame of mind; she wanted to find those old friendships. Not Gemma, however. Gemma was the only other one who had not married, Gemma had various scandalous liaisons with other people's husbands. People would try to team her up with Gemma. Exactly for that reason she had no interest in Gemma.

"She'd love to hear from you."

"Maybe I'll get a chance when I've finished unpacking," she said. She'd been close to her mother, always, but since she'd arrived home she was constantly irritated by her. "Look," she said angrily, "I tried the only person I cared about and it didn't work." She put down the phone, her stomach churning.

She walked over to the dormer window which made an alcove in her living room. She was a tenant in the attic of the kind of old house she had grown up in. The house had been painted and papered and divided into "heritage" apartments, although only fifteen years had passed since she left. Surely things happened too quickly in this town. Everything was a mistake, including the apartment. It had reminded her of a Toronto apartment, that was why she had taken it. But in Calgary it didn't seem so choice; it made her feel as if she couldn't afford anything better.

From the window she could see over to the riverside park where she and Lyall and Joey had played kick the can on long summer evenings. The light lasted until ten o'clock, sometimes later, and their voices had carried in the twilight with what seemed even then to be a sorrowful timbre. They had hated having to go in after dark. One night they arranged to sneak out and come back to the park at two in the morning.

It had been her idea, more daring than she understood, at fourteen or fifteen. Joey had come into the yard and knocked softly on the window of her room, which was off the rumpus room. She had met him in the side alley, and they had walked in the middle of the empty road all the way there. The park was gloriously dark, the dew forming. They set out across the damp grass; they could see a red light over by the trees. As they came closer they could make out Lyall, his bicycle up-side down, spinning the wheels, and the reflector glowing.

They came together breathless, uncertain of what to do. Away from the houses and the street the dark settled around them and became transparent, like a day from which all else had fled. They had never seen the middle of the night, outside, before. Their parents would kill them if they found out they were gone. It became necessary to do something to make this meeting worthy of its attendant risks.

They walked in single file between birches which looked a painted white, and found a picnic table, the kind made of heavy planks with benches attached. They'd spent an hour moving it twenty feet over to the bank. Then they had pushed it over so that it splashed into the water. They watched it bob up on an angle, like a bottle, and float away, and then they went home.

It was for such pranks that Lyall and Joey got the name of the bad boys. Lyall whined and had asthma attacks and endless enthusiasm for crime; Joey was blond and chubby and could carry anything off. In their grade five class Suzanne had laughed when he threw wads at the teacher but when he went to the principal's office to get the strap she remained demurely in her front seat. From shame, she had not dared look at him when he swaggered back down the aisle, after. "Twenty times," he whispered. "She drew blood, but I never even winced. I told her it hurt her more than it hurt me. Then she cried."

You couldn't get Joey by punishing him; he'd been punished so often, bearing it had become a badge of courage. What Joey did for Suzanne was to tell her about the things he did, the things she didn't dare do. He stole and he drank and he spied on the adults. He knew whose father had dirty books and whose mother was drunk in the afternoon and who gave the black eye to the woman who worked in the corner store. Suzanne relied on him to explain these things.

By high school, Joey had turned out fat and aggressive. In grade ten his parents gave him an Italian motorbike, blue. The next year he had a car. After the graduation dance he was speeding along Elbow Drive at four in the morning; neither Lyall or Suzanne was with him then, they had new friends. The car went out of control and crashed into a telephone pole, and he was dead.

Dead, just like that. Even for a bad boy, death seemed an extreme punishment. Word got around the neighborhood by noon the day after. Suzanne was sent across the lane to express condolances to Joey's mother. It was a brilliant sunny noon. The woman was lying on the sofa in the den with the drapes closed, eating chocolates from a box. When Suzanne said she was sorry, Joey's mother just looked at her. "What do you think you're doing," she said, "walking around here alive?"

Suzanne left the house and walked home through the back lane. There was the place where the bad boys had tied her to the fencepost, back in grade six. She leaned on the post and cried. She didn't see Joey these days, but she still felt as if he explained the world to her. She wanted to know what he would have said about the pain, this time. "The glass stuck into my neck, my guts went all over the wheel, God reached in the window and took away my license?"

That was how he might describe it, but how would he explain it? When he first got his scooter, Joey had sat in this very lane, his short, fat legs in khaki trousers spread over the egg-shaped motor. "I can drive faster than anyone else," he said, "because I don't care what happens to me. That makes it easy."

"But I care what happens to you," Suzanne had said.

He nodded, but she could see it didn't make any difference. She had not understood him; then she had not wanted to be his friend. But now, when he was gone, she saw. He was doing what the characters did in short stories, their teacher said, he was giving out clues which only the ending would explain. Suzanne went home then and told her mother that Joey had warned her ahead of time that he was going to die. Her mother had taken her in her arms.

"People often seem to do that," her mother had said, "especially those who die young."

Die young? Suzanne had thought. But youth was not the issue. She had not yet accepted that they would all die sometime; she was shocked that Joey had died at all, that he had left the world rather than his boyhood.

Suzanne turned away from the view. The dishes were still in the sink, but she bent and began to unpack books. Starting one thing before finishing another had become a problem. She picked up a copy of *The Sun Also Rises*. English 383, 1968. On other campuses there were fee strikes and computer burnings but in Calgary it was still raccoon coats and team pennants, Jumping Jack Flash at the beer bashes. At a basketball game the cheerleaders were pushed off the floor by a gang of scraggy girls wearing gas masks and yelling about insults to women. It was during a discussion of this very book that Suzanne's professor had invited his students to lie down on the floor and touch each other.

She did it, wanting to giggle, at first. But from that prone position, and hands crisscrossed over her body, she had looked into the ceiling, and through it, and had realized that everything, everything was going to be very different than what she expected.

Suzanne dropped Hemingway, and pawed through the box, coming upon old Norton anthologies, editions of Shakespeare's plays, her frosh beanie, the gift spoon from a fraternity formal. She had walked out of the classroom that day, telling the professor that encounter was not for her. How did it happen then that the rest of them turned out normal, and she had gone away? Should she have laid down and let them touch her?

Anyway it did no good to carry all this stuff around with her. All the way east, and in and out of those third floors. Now she'd brought it all home again and she couldn't throw it out. Anyway she might reread things, and catch what she seemed to have missed the first time.

In 1968 Suzanne had been living with three other girls in a rented bungalow across from Motel Village, ten minutes from the campus. That fall there was a sudden frost while the leaves were still green and the birches had turned a full, fantastic orange. Lyall came up beside her one day and drew a marijuana cigarette out of his pocket. Suzanne remembered distinctly that she was annoyed; she was wearing knee socks and penny loafers and thought she would be immune to this. But Lyall was insistent. He drew long experienced breaths and didn't talk in between. "Something to tell you," he gasped.

They walked along the highway passing the cigarette back and forth. Suzanne felt nothing, and figured he was acting. He came into her house. One of her roommates had hung a poster of a maharishi on the living room wall. Lyall put his face up to the paper and began to count the tiny dots that made the colour. "I got my guitar run over in Banff," he said. "I threw it in front of a truck and the splinters flew out like arrows." He began to cry. Suzanne understood that he was missing Joey, and she comforted him. Perhaps he was trying to be Joey.

It was nearly a year later that her mother called to say that Lyall had come back from California very sick. She said they had found him in the park by the river, digging a hole. He had said he was trying to bury the bad Lyall. Suzanne's mother thought that was a crazy thing, she repeated it, a crazy thing. "We never called him bad," she said.

Suzanne went to visit him in the psychiatric ward. He entertained her rather grandly, bringing out his beadwork, and some poems. His face was fat because he was being treated with drugs. As far as Suzanne saw, none of it did him any good. Two things happened to him there; he met Bonnie, and he lost control of his mind. Bonnie was a nurse. She kept telling him he was going to be fine, and the more she told him, the more he told terrible stories. Boundaries seemed to have broken down in his mind; he bled words, awful words, private words. Suzanne particularly hated it when he told her how sexy Bonnie was and how she let him do this and that but not the other.

When he got out he took other drugs. He told Suzanne he could see the curvature of the earth, when he looked into the distance, and that once, in a public washroom on Banff Avenue he had seen his own dead face. He went back into the hospital. The shock treatments were an unusual choice, but the family was impatient; they wanted him cured, quickly. Shocks, Bonnie told Suzanne brightly, were meant to eradicate certain bad memories that were depressing him. When he came out he was soggy, like a log which had begun to burn but had been doused with water.

When Bonnie and Lyall were married there were three bridesmaids, each with a different floral print in her dress. After the ceremony, the guests danced on the patio of Lyall's family's house, in front of the tennis court. All of the old neighbours were there. Even Joey's mother was there, healed up, sealed up, drinking a lot of champagne.

You'd never have known that anything had changed since the children were really children.

Suzanne stacked the books neatly on the floor beside the boxes. None of them had taught her what she needed to know. She was not giving up on them, but she wasn't sure if she wanted them in the room. There must be a book somewhere that said how you were supposed to feel when you were no longer young, but you were not yet dead; when something illegitimate, something you were never meant to have in the first place, like endless youth, or another woman's man, was taken away from you. She had never found such a book. She went back to the kitchen sink. The water was murky and cool.

She had seen Lyall only twice between his wedding day and today. The first time was when she came home to visit after she tried telling the married man she wouldn't see him again. Bonnie and Lyall had lived further out then, near Chinook Mall. The two women, never friends, walked on a frozen patch of grass by the children's skating rink. Suzanne fought disdain for Bonnie; it was not the decade for being a housewife. Bonnie sensed it. "The children need me, Lyall needs me," she said defensively. "But I always know I can do fine on my own if anything happens to him."

Suzanne resented that. The implication was that Lyall was fragile, or spoiling, and she would not betray him by believing it. But later he came to her city, alone. She had gone back to seeing the married man then, and was in love. Lyall talked about racing a motorcycle. He talked about going back to the land, about making films. Suzanne was mystified by these urges: what was it he so desperately needed to express? She couldn't remember anything original in him, even before his treatments.

In a hotel bar done up to resemble a library, Lyall drank a good deal. The stories began to come, as she had known they would. Once, he claimed, he had made Bonnie drive him miles over back roads, forcing her to get out every few miles so he could hit her. The way he got her to do it was by telling her he would kill her if she didn't, he confessed with a giggle.

Like a lot of things Lyall had said, the boast seemed only half true, but the truth and the lie mixed became doubly depressing. Suzanne sat there wondering what Joey would have done, if he'd lived. Joey might have become a middle-aged wife beater, and she would have hated him. But he was too smart for that, he had understood all of this from the beginning, and that was why he said he hadn't cared. He had cared, only his caring had taken the form of recklessness inviting death.

It was frightening, how she longed for Joey all these years. Lyall was a poor substitute. Back in her apartment she stared at the wall where the old plaster cracked in a jagged line between the windows. If Lyall wasn't crazy then he must be sane. First she pitied Bonnie and then she blamed her. Then she decided she'd never see either of them again.

But now she had come home. She put the last of the dishes up and let the water run out of the sink. She paced the apartment from one side to the other. There seemed to be nowhere to sit. She'd never bothered much with furniture. Maybe now that she was home for good she would start buying things.

She began kicking the empty cartons toward the stairs. She kicked them hard, and liked the noise. So much of her had been kept in, waiting. The affair was over. Her twenties were over, her escape was over. She had come home and she had been reduced to needing Lyall, Lyall who had always needed her and Joey so much more.

What she thought about then was Lyall's drugs, Lyall's shock treatments, Lyall's rushed cure. She had never dared to ask him how much he had forgotten. What she wanted to ask him today was if he remembered the night they stole the park bench, the way it looked, bobbing silently eastward in the river. The carpet, the kids, and Bonnie had stopped her. And then the look on his face, when she poured her tea in the plant. He had forgotten it, at least forgotten the wonder of it. Forgotten all but some vestige. She was with the bad boy in his memory in some small way, a rustle under the bushes, a flicker in deep darkness, just enough to bring that twitch of fear to his face.

Suzanne was standing at the window, crying. Please let me have a friend here, let me have a life here, she thought. How had the past been taken away? Had the shocks done it, or the drugs administered later; perhaps the sweetness of Bonnie had done it. It could have been nothing more sinister than time, the natural death of brain cells. There were deaths and more deaths. This memory died fifteen years ago with Joey, and then again, later, in Lyall. That meant she was the only person who kept it. And that would be all right, she decided, wiping her eyes. She had a feeling she was going to live a long, long time.

The Night-tender

The Night-tender

Ellen dragged both suitcases up the long flight of stairs from the train to Princess Street, keeping a cautious eye on the old woman labouring behind her. At the top she set them down, one on either side of her polished leather boots. She pushed the strand of hair back from her brow and wondered what to do next. Hannah took the last few steps clinging to the handrail; she had had a coughing fit halfway up. She stood beside Ellen, her sagging tweed coat open although it was cold. Clearly, no one had been sent to meet them; Ellen thought that for a poet of Hannah's reputation, if not for herself, at least the courtesy was due. But she was used to being disappointed. She would think no more of it and take charge herself.

Around them lay Edinburgh, a thin, peaked place on hills. Ellen took it in, through her eyes, her pores, feasting on its foreignness in her hungry way. She loved travel; a kind of possessiveness came to her in a new city, as if she could make it hers, become assured of it like its natives were, instantly.

''We should get a taxi,'' she said. She waved for one, but none appeared.

The sky was a deepening indigo although bells had just rung out five o'clock.

''That pub looks nice,'' said Hannah.

Ellen said nothing. Under the circumstances, the pub would not do. At last, a taxi angled toward them. Ellen heaved the suitcases across the back seat, helped Hannah in, and finally slid in herself. She turned to her companion.

''Shall we ask the driver to take us up to the castle to see the view? You look like you want cheering up.''

''You can't see the castle,'' said the man, turning his car downhill. ''It's not open now. At five o'clock the army takes over.''

''Perhaps we could see the view in any case.''

''Perhaps you'd like to get shot.''

''No, that won't be necessary,'' murmured the old woman, holding tightly to the purse in her lap. She had had a few on the train.

In the hotel room, however, Hannah flung her handbag on the bed, a rash, clumsy statement: quite suddenly she lost faith in that bag with whatever was in it to help her. She sat down hard on a chair. Her feet lifted off the floor, bringing into sight her shoes, comic shoes with turned up toes and laces tied too tightly and thick high heels such as those worn by can-can dancers. Ellen felt she was in the presence of a passionate child rather than a well-known poet twice her age. Of this trip she had expected many things, not all of which were clear in her mind. She was certain, however, that they did not include playing nursemaid to the woman who had raised, decades earlier, such a bold clamour for the emancipation of her sex.

"I want a drink," Hannah said. "I *need* a drink."

"How about having some dinner before this reception? It'd do you good. I can take us somewhere nice. They'll pay." Ellen cocked her head in the general direction of the university. Being a doctor of philosophy and holding down a tenured position, having published several favourably reviewed books, she had more power with these establishments than did Hannah. There were times when Ellen found the ease with which the world worked for her embarrassing; this was one of them.

"Dinner?" sneered Hannah, pulling a nasty, alcoholic face.

Ellen turned her back, ashamed for Hannah. It was a bad feeling for her, since reverence had been her first response. When, as a student, she had first discovered H.L. Winters, she had traipsed up and down Bloor Street, searching the bookshops for the few works. That she, Ellen, was now in a position to introduce the long-lost poet at a government-sponsored conference on women writers was still an amazement to her. She was determined that it should be a success, but the words of that nasty agent who'd pointed her to Hannah's cottage in Devon came back to her.

"You get her there, my lovely," the agent had said, "if that's what you want. Get her there and you can have her."

"But what does *she* want? Would it please her?"

There had been no answer. "Is she writing?" she'd said, supplying the respect that was missing.

He snorted, "Oh no, she won't be doing that again."

"Dinner would be lovely," Hannah said suddenly, sweetly.

Ellen turned.

"Dinner *and* a drink."

"I'd like that too," said Ellen, relenting. "Shall we change first?"

"Change?" Hannah's look was full of scorn.

"Let me just go to my room and get ready. I'll be back in twenty minutes."

In her own room she found herself pacing. She felt grimy and tired, wanting a bath but unable to trust Hannah alone long enough to get one. Did she have a bottle? Hannah would have to eat; how else could she last until the reception? She stopped her fretful walk and began to unpack her bag. She pulled out the new purple dress she'd brought for the evening. It looked great on her, James had said. She put it on a hanger. She wouldn't wear it. She hoped to be unselfish and not to compete: she was patient and had time to be noticed, while Hannah had less. More than that, since meeting the older woman she'd become unsure whether women writers were supposed to wear attractive new purple dresses. She changed her shirt and looked quickly at her hair, wishing it was not so pale.

Hannah was exactly were she'd been left. "The handbag," she said.

Bending over the bed, Ellen retrieved the purse and delivered it to its owner. Hannah searched inside and found a brush. She pulled the pins from her thick, springy, grey-brown hair. It sprang out like the hair of a girl. She twisted it rather violently and put it back up again. She drew out a broken piece of mirror and held it in front of her mouth. She pursed her lips and with a new tube of lipstick slowly drew an outrageous red oval over their creases. Without blotting the lipstick, she put everything back in the purse and patted the lap of her black dress. It was a little too tight.

"There!" she said mockingly. "How do I look?"

It is not altogether my fault, Ellen thought, this need you acknowledge to be presentable. You've gone along with it, in a way; you've kept close to the shore. This was the critic speaking. The convent school, the society manners with which you draw people in for the pleasure of shocking them later with your revolts — scandals, debauches, poverty, drunkenness. It gave the work its special poignancy. But the woman? She reached for her own lipstick.

"You look great. I'm sure you'll be a big hit."

Hannah did not seem to hear. Her old eyes, yellowed, clotted, fierce with expectation, searched Ellen's depths. Ellen turned away disquieted.

Henderson's had been recommended for dinner. Again Ellen made the mistake of asking their taxi driver.

"You're no vegetarians, are you? You'll get carrot soup there." He suggested the Luckpenny.

"Can you get a drink there?"

"So it's a drink you're wanting, is it?" He turned and stared rudely at Hannah, taking in the reddened nose, the nervous squint, and shaking hands. Ellen saw him conclude that she was a pitiable drunk. From where she sat Ellen could also see the shoes, the soiled coat, and too-tight dress. She wanted to shout "for God's sake she's a great poet, who cares if she looks like everyone else?" At the cottage, in her Wellingtons and working smock, Hannah had looked perfect. Perhaps it had been cruel to bring her away.

"Terrible man," said Hannah, as they stepped out of the taxi.

"They're coming out of the woodwork," said Ellen.

The Luckpenny looked promising; Egon Ronay had visited. The women sat and immediately got their drinks, spirits for Hannah and wine for Ellen.

"Cheers!" said Ellen. But Hannah already had her face in her tumbler. When she lifted it she looked straight at Ellen.

"So are you prepared for success?"

"For what? Oh well, I don't expect it." Ellen laughed, uncomfortable at the direction of the conversation, Besides, it was Hannah's night.

"Can't be avoided," persisted Hannah.

"Shall we get some food?"

Hannah frowned and stubbed out her cigarette too energetically, smashing it into the shape of a crumpled tire. "I'll not do any more writing, it's up to you." You don't mean that, thought Ellen, but it may just be true.

As she drew another cigarette from the package, her hands shook. The calloused and tobacco-stained fingers, like some root vegetable freshly pulled from the earth and scrubbed raw, were of such compelling reality that between them the cigarette was white and thin, a phantom. Ellen watched as the physical reality took over from and vanquished the imaginary writer she'd worshipped. This was Hannah, who had spent her life feeding children, washing, planting, with no man to help. For the first time she wondered if Hannah had had to make things so hard for herself.

As Hannah looked around for someone to light her cigarette, a young waiter stepped forward. The match flared. Hannah leaned toward him, the arch of her brow and the drag of her breath acknowledging his nearness and his maleness.

"What do you do," she said, sucking in air, "are you a student?"

"Art student," he said.

"Of course," she said. "I can see it. You've got a sensuous face." Her cheeks drawn in, her eyes wide, Hannah changed in that instant from an out-of-breath old woman twisting the waist of her dress to someone young, shocking, dangerous.

Eyes popping, the waiter backed off. Hannah removed the cigarette from her mouth. "Lovely young man," she remarked. Ellen sat up straighter.

"Smoke?"

"I don't."

"No, of course, you wouldn't; you're too healthy."

"I never could get the hang of it. I guess I have no decadence in me."

"I noticed something like that," said Hannah. She beckoned the waiter for more drink. "But how do you get along? I don't know if I could get through anything at all without a few drinks," she said. "I've thought of giving up drink, but if I did, I'd have to give up people, too."

"Surely not all of us?" said Ellen, with a smile. She did hope to be blessed by her heroine, but the possibilities seemed to be growing slimmer. For one thing, she was not exactly all there. Her wealth had been mined already, strip-mined, leaving the surface rough and unregenerative. She was mined also, thought Ellen, allowing herself a literary game, as in planted through with tiny bombs.

Last night, which they had spent together at the cottage, had been magic. True, before Hannah had got warmed up there had been a stiffness. And after she'd got too warmed, there had been an incomprehensible outburst at an unnamed faithless lover and a shoulder of lamb in flames in the oven. After it had been extinguished, and a dinner of potatoes served to Ellen (Hannah did not eat), more raging. Finally Ellen had had to push her up the stairs to bed. All of this had been frightening, and yet the worst had been after, during the night, when the awful sounds had come from Hannah's room — jumbled shouts and bellows like an animal in pain. But somewhere in there there had been an hour or two of splendid, luminous conversation. Ellen thought she would do anything for those few hours again.

"I'm thinking of having children," she said suddenly.

"Don't do anything until you have to," muttered Hannah. "Let life take you by storm," she said. Her mouth hung open. "I wanted to be taken over, possessed. I wanted children to swarm over the bed."

"Have to?" said Ellen. "That doesn't happen any more. I don't know what you mean." Nothing was going to take her by storm. James, perhaps, but only when she permitted him to. She filled her wine glass again.

"Perhaps you should find out," said Hannah tartly. "It would do your writing good."

Ellen drained the glass. She was astonished at how this criticism — surely it was criticism — hurt. She wanted so much to show Hannah who she was — a writer too. Did an instinct for self-preservation disqualify her? She bit her lip and looked over her shoulder for the waiter. "We've got to eat."

Hannah was watching her very closely. "You aren't in any kind of despair, are you?"

"No. Certainly not."

They both got another drink. It was seven-thirty. Hannah decided she would eat, but it was too late. The restaurant was closing. The couples with their frizzy children and the patched students were leaving. The dark young waiter began to move quickly around the tables near them, wiping, whistling. He had a smile on his face, thinking about his sensuousness, no doubt. Soon all of the other patrons were gone. Ellen thought they really ought to be going to the reception. But they were having such a lovely time. Conversation had at last begun to come, conversation about music, about books, about women.

"I was the first one out," said Hannah. "Before me all the women writers had no children. I wanted to see if it could be done."

"And you're living proof?"

For an answer, Hannah held up her handbag into which she'd packed the two thin volumes of poetry. That was all. "I always said I'd get back to it."

The waiter lifted up the chairs and set them on top of the tables. Now there were only four chairs on the floor — Ellen's, Hannah's and the two empty ones near them. Ellen refused to be thrust again into the custodial role; she decided to say nothing about the time. Up came the young waiter to take his turn.

"Time to go, ladies."

"What?" said Hannah. "So early? That's rather mean, isn't it? What do you have to do? Go home and get some sleep?" She patted the empty chair. "Can't we have a little chat? A party? What do you do about your despair?"

"I close up by eight, ma'am."

Hannah focussed her contempt. "How very boring, young man."

"If you say so, ma'am."

After the reception which had been filled with fans of Hannah's and was a great success for her, except for the curious fact that she refused to speak when asked to address the crowd, they were dropped off at their hotel. It was still not late, and Hannah did not want to go in. They linked arms and took a turn around St. Andrew's Square. Ellen's worry had all been for nought: Hannah had behaved like a professional. Mind you, a watchful don had pulled away her wine glass, but Hannah had been involved in autographing a book and hadn't noticed. Ellen felt heady; the day had been long, but the success of the venture and the drinks made her want to skip and run. Suddenly Hannah dropped on her side to the grass, which was thick with little pearls of condensation. She rolled as if suffering from cramp.

"Agh, agh," she cried, jabbing her fingers into her hair.

"Get up, Hannah," said Ellen. There was no response. She got down on her knees beside the old woman. "I really hate being your nurse," she said aloud.

Hannah stopped and sat, perfectly lucid. "Then don't be. I can take care of myself. You're not my mother. You're not even my daughter." Then she went on pulling her hair, prying out the pins, shaking her head until the thick youthful strands sprang up. "Agh, agh, they were pulling my leg, weren't they? They were."

"No they weren't. Don't you remember the redhead? She could recite practically the whole prologue. They were admirers, Hannah, they love your work."

"Where were the boys?"

"They're feminists. Aren't girls good enough?"

"What do they want with me? Why do they ask about my life? I have no advice."

"You said you were the first one out." Of this Ellen herself was not convinced; all night in the back of her mind she had been composing a list of other women writers of Hannah's time who'd had children. But this was not the time to argue. "They want to know how you do it. They want to know (Ellen knew she was venturing into dangerous ground, but ventured nonetheless) why it stopped."

"Feminists and scholars," Hannah was muttering. "Such terrible people. Did you see that man take away my glass? How dare he? No one even knows how to be civil. Afraid that I might speak the truth."

Ellen managed to get her off the grass and turned back toward the hotel. They passed the flat pink faces of life insurance buildings. In the bottom of one was a bride's shop, featuring a mannequin all done up with a tiara. Hannah stopped.

"You see? That was all I ever wanted."

Ellen laughed.

"That's good," said Hannah, "do that more."

Ellen laughed again, self-conscious.

"All you modern women are so serious. You should drink more. Stay up all night. Drinking too much is very important, you know."

As they turned the corner the wind came at them; there was a hump of a hill and then their hotel, the railroad tracks beyond and the bridge, and across the bridge the tenements, square, cut to match the hills like Inca cliff dwellings. They braced up, drawing their coats more tightly around them. It began to rain. Laughing like girls they skittered along the sidewalk and entered the hotel. The descent into incoherence had been staved off again. Ellen was complimented; Hannah was staying with her in order to make contact; she had decided that Ellen was one of them. Ellen would try to live up to the judgement.

"Nightcap?" said Hannah brightly.

"Why not?"

Shaking the raindrops off their coats, Hannah and Ellen burst into the Residents' Lounge. It was a long room with tall graceful windows on three sides through which, across the murky sky halved by turrets and cupolas, Arthur's Seat could be seen brooding over the city. The ceiling was high, grandly corniced with plaster flowers and eggs. The walls and floor alike were in musty rose of various textures. Around the edges of the room ran a single row of straight-backed, narrow chairs. Three of these chairs were occupied. In one a man hid himself, save for grey pant legs, behind a copy of *The Scotsman*. Opposite him, a young couple stolidly held hands and regarded a nearly silent television.

"My goodness, a roomful of stiffs," said Hannah. "Where are the drinks?"

Ellen giggled. Then she turned around in search of the bar service they'd been told was available. On one wall stood a vending machine. She went up to inspect. It was a dusty metal box about the size of a refrigerator with various slots and trays and windows. There was a sign at eye-level. *Night-tender*, it said. Not for use by persons under 18.

"Come look," she said. "It's just what we need. Someone pleasant to pour the drinks, and he stays on late."

"Isn't he sweet!" said Hannah. "What does he need?"

There was a slot calling for two ten-pence pieces, and under it, a glass window showing corked vessels of spirits. "Glasses," surmised Ellen. "He must want glasses."

She ran out of the room with Hannah's key and then back again to her own room, returning with two glasses to find Hannah squatting on the floor in front of the *Night-tender*, trying to see into the opening. She had two coins in her fingers.

"Stand back," said Ellen. "I'll do it." She read from the metal tag under the coin slot. "Insert coin above and turn key clockwise. Check that optic is full and *Sold Out* light is not illuminated."

"*Sold Out* light. Oh dear. But it isn't on. Nothing is on."

A voice came from behind the book. "It's no working."

"No working? Oh surely he is, he looks brand new, only wants a bit of dusting," said Hannah brightly. She whirled in the centre of the room with a tottery grace in her ridiculous shoes and then approached the *Night-tender* beguilingly. Humming a tune, she jiggled it, prodded and nudged it in a friendly way. She fumbled with her coin at the opening, and when she couldn't get it in, held her arms up, akimbo, as if to dance with it. Ellen sang along with her tune, but, knowing that the practical side had been assigned to her, stopped to snatch up the telephone which hung on the wall beside the machine.

"Hello?"

"Yes. I'm in the lounge and the *Night-tender* doesn't seem to be working."

"What's that?"

"The drink machine. Is it working?"

"Oh, I see. Well, have you had a go at it?"

"The lights won't come on." Ellen heard her own voice as if from across the room. It was a querulous, 'American' voice, the voice of a girl no longer a girl, of a woman who wanted her nightcap badly, although she'd had plenty already. It occurred to her that, to others, she and Hannah were virtually of a type.

"Perhaps the plug is out. Look down along the bottom of the table there, to the right. See if you can find the switch."

"Hold on." She passed the telephone to Hannah and got down on her hands and knees. A fat, grey rubber-covered wire and a triangular plug lay on the carpet. Ellen put in the plug. Hannah handed back the receiver.

"Now."

"Put the glass under the spout. What happens?"

Nothing happened. The voice on the phone was fading. "Well, did you put in your coins?"

The coins would not enter the slot. The machine was still, dumb, yet to be put in motion. Hannah, tired of gentler ministrations, began bashing it with her shoulder. The couple watching television clenched hands and looked at each other in embarrassment.

"Wait," said the man at the other end of the telephone. "Did you switch it on?"

"Switch it on?" said Ellen. "Oh yes, of course." She was lying. She'd forgotten the British paranoia about electricity leaking out of open switches. She got down on her hands and knees again, cradling the receiver with her chin, and flipped a switch on the outlet. Hannah's pleasure with the machine had turned to rage; she seemed to confuse it with some faithless lover. "And you said, get out of here, you old bugger, and so I said not on your —"

"You'll no get it working," opined the grey-pants man, lowering his paper.

"Hold it," said Ellen, "I'm getting there." Dusting off her hands, she stood up and looked at the brown box. There was a click and a shudder as the current went on. Then a bright orange light beamed out, *Sold Out*. They both groaned.

Ellen picked up the phone again. "It says *Sold Out* now," she said bitterly into the receiver. She had a feeling that her instructor at the other end had known all along it would.

"Oh well," he said. "I guess it is, then."

"Agh, agh, agh," said Hannah, pulling one of the chairs out of the line along the rim of the room and dropping onto it. Her lips pursed and grinned, alternately; she pulled her eyebrows down and then lifted them in astonishment. She banged the back of her head on the wall.

I can handle this, thought Ellen. She made her voice more firm. "Look, can we get drinks sent up to us here then? Would there be someone who could bring them up?"

"That would be me I guess," said the man, sadly, admitting defeat.

"Fine," she said. "We'll have two brandies in the lounge." She replaced the receiver loudly.

"I got them!" she announced triumphantly to Hannah.

"You did? Oh, you did!" Perhaps Hannah had forgotten all about the nightcap which she did not need, but she recognized Ellen's triumph. "Bully for you!" She raised up her elbow, offering a swing, and Ellen pulled her out of the chair. The two women twirled each other in the middle of the room. This at last was too much for the company; the grey pant legs uncrossed, and the man behind the book pushed himself to his feet.

"I'll say good-night then," he announced, as if concluding a long chat.

"Good-night," chimed Hannah and Ellen. As he left, their eyes turned to the couple watching television. No such luck. They didn't look as if they were ever going to stir.

"Men! They're all the same," said Ellen after the sulky little man had brought their drinks and gone away handsomely tipped and no less annoyed.

"They're afraid of you, I expect," said Hannah.

"They are not!" said Ellen indignantly. "James isn't."

"He wants to have children too?"

"He does if I do." That was not exactly true. In fact James had said that he could not imagine having children with Ellen and that Ellen was not the sort of woman any man would be willing to settle down with. He had said that Ellen was the sort of woman men had as a mistress. They had quarrelled bitterly over this, and Ellen did not even know if, when she got back home, they would see one another again. "Why should they be afraid of me? I'm no danger. I don't ask for anything out of the ordinary. Just a little looking after. Just like you do."

"You can't have it all."

"You had it."

"Oh no, I did not. I certainly did not."

"Men, books, children. Success." Although of the last, Ellen was somewhat uncertain. Before she met Hannah she'd have said it, but closer up, things were not so clear.

"But look at me now. Look at what I have left. See?" Hannah raised her arms. The seams in the tight black dress were popping. "For my pains. Nothing." She shook the hair out of her eyes. They glittered now, they were no longer yellow, but sparkling, as if they had been bathed in acid. "You must expect nothing, then you will never be bitter."

Ellen jumped. Tears came to her eyes. How did Hannah know about her bitterness, which she was so careful to conceal? It was an ugly word, but what she felt really was a kind of bitterness, the bitterness of having jumped ship and forsworn safety, and of having your absence go unrecorded. Taken for granted as one who rode into the eye of the storm and managed to stay alive, but resentful of having to do that job for all the safe others. There was the other matter too of Hannah's own bitterness which was obvious, her constant observation of the hatefulness of others.

"Anyway," said Hannah, passing the brandy under her nose, "you'll have no reason to be bitter. You'll do it all. You'll be able to slip through. If it's not James, then another. Don't you think I see what kind of person you are?"

"I don't know what you mean." Ellen had wanted

Hannah to see into her, but not to see this. ''You think so little of me?''

''On the contrary. I admire you very much,'' said Hannah. She grimaced and blinked her eyes, fast. Ellen's mouth fell open at the rude parody of herself. Hannah got to her feet, stumbling in her loose shoes. ''I do have something to say. I just couldn't say it there, tonight, in front of those people.''

The couple watching television nodded to each other and stood up suddenly to leave. Hannah raised her voice to stop them.

''What I have to say is this. It is impossible to be a woman writer, impossible because of the need for man. You see,'' she said to the captured couple, ''the cock is unable to rise up in face of woman's words.'' She drew her glass to the side of her nose. ''The feminist speaks,'' she concluded and laughed.

Ellen slowly pulled herself to her feet and, holding her glass against her lip, made ready to answer. The remark had to be debated, surely. She couldn't let it stand. And yet, she couldn't muster the strength to argue.

''That's bullshit,'' she said impotently.

Hannah laughed again.

Ellen wavered on her feet. She'd had more to drink than she realized. The young couple, looking from one woman to the other, took advantage of their stand-off to turn to the door. When it shut behind them, a certain energy went out of Hannah and Ellen's confrontation. They both backed onto chairs.

''Another one?''

''Oh no, I couldn't.''

''I couldn't either. It keeps me awake.''

''We should go to bed.''

"We should. But I'll sit up a bit." said Ellen.

"You've been very kind," said Hannah.

"Though not in the right way," said Ellen.

"Well," said Hannah. "Don't worry."

"Good-night, Hannah; sleep well."

"Yes, you too. Good-night then."

They kissed. Hannah opened the door and went out, quite sober, taking the whole evening with her. Ellen sat back on her stiff chair. In her mind she played out the rest of the night. She would go to bed and read until she was tired. She would close her eyes and hope to sleep. If she did not sleep, she would be very, very quiet so as not to disturb anyone. So as not to disturb Hannah in the next room. She told herself this caution was ridiculous: Hannah didn't care. Hannah would be sound asleep, tossing and crying the way she had that night in Devon; her torment, her "despair", as she liked to call it, dominant, indulged.

Ellen growled suddenly with pain and pressed her fists against her eyes. Tonight more than ever she knew how she was drawn to that fitful bed and repelled by it. But she'd made her decision. She would hide her own despair, and half the time she would forget that it was there. The baby issue could wait, too; she would use the summer to get some poems done. And if, as Hannah said, it wasn't James, then it would be someone else.

The Dancer

The Dancer

She worked her feet down into the hot sand. The earth was minimal there: sky, land, ruff of sea, caw of bird high over the water. Behind Anna the sun came to a bank of cloud and entered it, changing the colour of everything. All through the mapless jungle at her back, fleshy leaves darkened from green to the colour of blood. Shade passed like wind over the water, raising its crystal to turquoise. It spread across the sand and along the beach which ran out of an oily harbour to the bazaars. It darkened the doors of the flat-roofed, open-mouthed houses that were for the town's rich, passed through the poor stick huts on the outskirts and in seconds had laid itself along the promontory beach so that the skin hairs rose and the brows furrowed on the tourists who suntanned in front of their aqua-tinted hotel. But Anna, whose skin was already a dusky tan, did not miss the sun that minute. She dug the knife edges of her feet deeper into the sand. She was a dancer, and she had been on her way somewhere else.

No one had ever thought she would be a dancer. Her parents were European peasants, cousins who'd escaped their village in a fit of courage before the war, thinking to enact their marriage on the hard bed of the Canadian prairies. Once there, they'd caught fear from the land. Its breadth was such that they could not imagine farming. They huddled in the creases of a small town, working for other people. Anna was born to them late, a child who was the colour of the dust that came through the doorsill. Her skin stretched over great cradles of bones that seemed to grow faster than her flesh. Adult at fourteen, her pelvis hollow and hard like an animal skull half-buried in the tufted prairie dirt, that was Anna. Her legs were wide apart and thin. All collar-bone and elbow, with an exceptional darkness in her eyes and the inside of her mouth, the child only added to her parents' countless worries. She wanted dance lessons, and although she was plain and awkward compared to the fair-skinned, pug-nosed children who filled the dance school, Anna's parents decided she would have them. Perhaps the dancing would make her happier. She was not considered a talent. Anna was strange and secretive; no one in the town knew what she was feeling.

The day she left, mounting the three tin steps to a train going east, it seemed that all concerned had simply been waiting the twenty years of Anna's life for the departure. Her parents waved goodbye and turned away when she'd disappeared into the car. In the latter years their daughter had become an intruder in their conspiracy to survive. Anna sat up in the coach all the long afternoon and evening, until the sun set behind her back and she could not see anything. Her eyes were open when it rose again, straight in front of her where the tracks led. She got off in Toronto and without difficulty found a furnished room, a job in a dry-goods store, and a dancing school.

In the dancing school they danced in bare feet. It was modern dance, something the rest of the world had known for forty years. Her wide feet no longer captured in box-like slippers, Anna came free into a new continent of movement. Instead of tunics and hairnets and ribboned slippers, she wore loose terry-cloth pants and heavy socks with the toes and heels cut away so that the balls of her feet and her heels made a flesh connection with the hardwood floors. The movements she was taught were grounded and hieroglyphic. Instead of pointing and twirling like a useless toy, she sat spread-legged, gripping the floor, rolling into it, stretching and cocking her limbs. Flat-footed, she used her weight and the looseness of her joints. She learned about contracting and releasing her body from the spring in her pelvis. She danced as she never had before. And yet there was something familiar to her in each mastery of a new movement. She was discovering her dream self, a self that had existed earlier, sliding, coiling, and darting on some brilliant mental slate. The challenge was to make her body correspond to her imagination. She worked every day, diligently. Within the year she was dancing with reptilian grace.

After three years of this training Anna quit her job as a clerk and joined the company as a junior. There were ten dancers, all young and living in the style of the urban poor. Two men — Terry, tall and weedy with a spray of dry hair and Richard, compact and positive as a pistol — came as near to being friends with Anna as anyone did. She moved into a house with them, and they lived like brothers and sister. From the women in the company Anna learned to live everything through her body; with that loose, earthbound quality she made love casually, as if she were in rehearsal. What history and innocence she might have had she lost. She began to seem much like the others, who came out of private schools and show business families. She slept sometimes with men and sometimes with women, but she kept company mainly with her wiry black dog which she acquired from a drunk woman in a subway station. Nights when she was not rehearsing, which were few, she went to movies alone.

She had lived like that for five years, years when she'd been licked by her own sweat and soothed by the uninformed applause of the audience. She moved up in the small hierarchy of the company, taught a few classes, and went on a few tours. She began to see younger students gaze at her with large envious eyes, but she was barely aware that her life could seem something wonderful. She lived with a sense of displacement; she never spoke of where she came from. It was hard to believe that the town still existed. But she was uneasily aware that what she had now might be undeserved. She dreamt that it was taken away from her, and she was left bowlegged and unable to move her feet from the ground on the edge of a prairie schoolyard. But she woke up and knew she wanted nothing else but to go on with it. In infrequent letters to her parents she told them she was dancing with a company and felt that they would disapprove. She was twenty-eight.

That summer, eight years after Anna had seen the prairie, the company travelled to Mexico City to do a series of performances at the university. Standing beside a car rental booth in the big airport, Anna had looked at a map of the country. Mexico seemed to her glittering, treacherous. She had an idea she'd take a holiday. She'd defect. There was an island across from the eastern coast. She liked its shape, like a footprint half washed away. It was called Isla

Mujeres because, as the guide she asked told her, it was the place where pirates used to take the women they'd made captive. Anna nodded to him and walked away from her group without being noticed, took a bus to Veracruz and then to Mérida, another bus to Puerto Juárez, from there a ferry, and finally after two dreamless days, she arrived at her island. As the ferry drew to shore, she saw that the rocks on the ocean side were black and that knotted short trees grew by the water's edge. The coastal side of the island was more tame. At the hotel Anna cashed her travellers' cheques and received an astonishing number of pesos. She went through the bazaars and bought three silver and turquoise rings, all of which she put immediately on her fingers, a white smock embroidered in the Yucatan style, and some very expensive plums and apples. She meant to expend all her extravagances at once so that she would not be bothered by them again. She paid a week's rent on a small thatch roofed hut adjacent to the hotel. There was a lot of money left.

It was less a vacation than a period of waiting. She had stayed in her hut most of the time, lying on the cot or in the hammock or sitting in the woven chair with her feet on a stool, looking over rocks she'd gathered on the beach, eating the creamy, sour melons that were plentiful, and rereading an escaped *Village Voice* she had found on the beach. Evenings she went into town to eat, walking down the dusty road and startling lizards back into the undergrowth. She did not speak to any of the stocky Mexicans who would pull out the chair for her at the café table, or to the denim-clad crap throwers with black coral finger rings. In the mornings, wearing her dance leotards and terry pants, she'd go out onto the tier of hard sand above the beach to do warm-ups.

She began by standing erect, staring out to sea. Then, shifting only one foot, she folded herself carefully to sit straightbacked, her knees opening to make a cradle. Then she put the soles of her feet together and gripped her ankles with her hands. She let her breath out and turned the base of her spine under, dropping her head to stretch. Her long back licked forward and back and sideways over captive limbs. Then she would straighten her back and split her legs apart like knives, bending forward until she lay protracted between them. She rolled onto her back and contracted her pelvis and stomach, letting her head fall back so that her neck tendons stood out to the sun and the insides of her arms pressed upwards. That exercise was called the pleading. The warm sand gave under her, shifted, fed back to her weight as if it were a live partner. After she worked her muscles into warmth, she would sit cross-legged and still, baking in the glare of the Caribbean sun. She might have been some ancient jewelled lizard in her wary rest, some lizard whose slick eye could, in an hour or a day, flicker, its body grip the earth and be gone.

The boy was there one morning when she stood, stretching out the tendons in the back of her legs and looking up from a half hour's work-out. He had a rake in his hand and was leaning on it, the flat end buried in sand. He smiled.

''Beautiful,'' he said, making it a very long word.

Anna looked away, but she had no impulse to stop. She was missing the studio mirrors, and she was glad of the company of his eyes. She finished her stretch and then began to run along the beach slowly, in low, loose strides, her body upright and steady as a beam of light sweeping the horizon.

The boy came back the next day and watched. Later, during the small hot death of the siesta, he came to her hut.

She was sitting in front in the shade.

"Please," he had said, and they went into Anna's hut and lay down together. Their skin was dry and slid like fabric over their lean muscles. Anna was slow to become excited, and he stood up to leave before she realised she wanted him.

"Thanks, lady," he said as he left. He looked very solemn. Anna knew only then that he had almost no English.

He came back to see her day after day. He brought new English words to court her. He told her she was a golden angel. After they made love he told her about himself. His name was Salvador. He was twenty-one years old and had eight years of schooling and two years in the military. He had many brothers and sisters, but they did not live here on the island. He had come here to stay with his aunt because there had been no place for him at home after he'd come back from the army. Anna said nothing about herself except that she was from Canada. Salvador had imagined that she was praying when he had first seen her on the beach. Anna told him that she danced, but she didn't dance for him again.

She stayed almost two months in the grass-roofed hut, washing herself in the washroom in the hotel lobby, giving her laundry to the chambermaids to take home, and eating in the cafés every night. She felt rich and careless. By then she and the boy Salvador walked together in the streets and drank beer at the *Cervecia*. Salvador had adopted the habit of hanging a toothpick off the lower lip in the fashion of a French intellectual he'd seen pictured in Anna's *Village Voice*. They walked arm in arm and she wore her long red skirt under the white smock. Salvador nodded and spoke to the smallish wide-bodied men and women with their round faces and chopped away eyes and noses. The evenings when Salvador worked for a friend who had some vague business operation, Anna would go for dinner alone in town as she had done before they met. Eating refrillo and drinking coffee out of a glass, Anna would sit in the café darkened by the early sunset and sometimes speak to the boys who came to sit by her asking after Sal. She became a part of the place without knowing it. All at once she realised that she and Salvador had a language between them, made up of hers and his and covering the present and the necessary. That was about the time that she came to the end of her money.

She had not known what to do. First she thought she'd carry on and not tell the boy. But with no more of those large coins, she could not buy fruit or beer for dinner. He noticed, of course, and brought her some rolls and packaged cheese and green and orange melon from the hotel. He gave her a water pouch. He didn't believe that her supply of pesos had dried up completely; perhaps he thought she was merely resting before she began to produce them again, like loaves and fishes, from the few he was able to give her. Anna had not gone to the desk at the hotel to pay her rent for that week. It was several days later when the clerk, who was a friend of Salvador, came to where she sat wrapped in her shawl with the purple blossoms on it in the shade of her hut and asked her for the money.

"I have no money," said Anna, in English. She did not wish to be as personal with him as to speak his language. She felt very distant. She faced the sea and could almost have forgotten him, but for his shuffling. The clerk smiled. He did not believe her. He asked if she had credit cards. North Americans did not need to have money, they could show cards and have their charges put off. But Anna did not have cards. At length the clerk went away. When he came back with the manager, Anna was still sitting in that shady spot, fingering the sand. She offered to work at the hotel, but the manager told her it was not possible because she was a tourist. So when Salvador came to meet her that afternoon, Anna had packed her duffle, leaving the *Voice* behind, and was sitting above the beach quite homeless.

Finally, Salvador understood that she had no more money. He felt then that he loved her very much and was proud that she had placed herself in his hands. He took her to a white-washed adobe hut with no doors, set in the back of town, in the yard of a larger adobe hut which faced the foot road that ran away from the back of the town toward the jungle. In this place dogs ran, the occasional skinny Brahman bull meandered, and leggy chickens scavenged. Anna missed the sea there. Sometimes Salvador stayed overnight with her, but more often he went back to his aunt's house. She did not sleep well then. She woke frightened as the long dawn came through her open doorway and the dogs loped up to sniff. She'd get up early and go to the well in the courtyard to wash out her clothes in a basin borrowed from the neighbor. Then she'd take her bag and walk to the sand by the harbour to do her exercises. She did not think much about how this had come to pass or how it might end. She waited for Salvador; when he was there it did not seem strange. To be poor in a foreign place was an experience which did not surprise Anna.

Those were the days when she sat on the sand in front of the low and silent Mexican town in the heat of midday and thought about where she'd come from. Not of the people she'd recently left, but of her old home. Her parents taught her the poverty that was powerless and ashamed, of cabbage soup for a week, the fear that meant putting a knife through the inside of a door latch because the lock did not work and someone might come to steal the week's pay, given in small bills. The worse fear of having nothing that could be stolen; the Fridays when her father came home without his pay because the employer had "forgotten."

This past made Anna scorn her next life, the dancer's stylish urban poverty. Rooms with cockroaches and dangling overhead fixtures, thin walls which repeated the creak and groan of wearying lovemaking, thrift-store shopping for old clothes now fashionable. That kind of being poor was mostly show; it had left money for the shoes that were currently deemed healthy — wooden sandals or suede scuffs with the heel set at an odd angle — and money for dinner in roof garden restaurants. For the others it had been a game, choreographed against the backrop of city and patrons and a bedroom kept up in the family home for emergencies. Here in Mexico she'd made herself wait for the poverty that pretended nothing, that accepted the double-edged abasement of begging. Anna dug her feet into the hot sand, bowed her head, and smiled her small victory.

Thinking of home made Anna miss her dog. She wished it could jump in front of her and rub its frizzy forehead on her knee. She decided to write a letter. She took some coins she might have bought coffee or beer with to the store and bought paper and envelopes. Back in the adobe hut she wrote about the shack and about Salvador, that he was young, that he had a criminal record (something she had just discovered), and that he sometimes worked as a gardener, and that she was living with him, which was not quite true.

"We are very poor," she found herself writing. "I don't know how we will manage. I cannot leave him." Anna sent the letter off to her own unfamiliar address with a signed cheque enclosed, asking for money out of her bank account. On the envelope she scribbled an inquiry about the dog. Because she had the paper, she wrote also to her parents. She had to beg Salvador for the money for stamps. After she'd mailed the letters, Anna went back to sitting in her spot on the beach.

Two months passed in the adobe hut, and then Anna realized she was pregnant. She knew this meant some kind of change, so she didn't tell Salvador. And then an answer to her letter came — a note from Terry urging her to come home. There was a money order enclosed, for more than she'd had in her account. The dangers of Mexico — jails, disease, bandits — were cited. Her room in the house was waiting, and her dog was missing her. No mention was made of her defection, of Salvador; the letter was casual and cheerful. From Terry's tone Anna understood that he thought she was crazy, that she might be frightened away if her behaviour was questioned. She wavered between gratitude and a feeling that her friend had failed her.

But Anna forgot about the letter as soon as she began to use the money. It was fortunate she had it, for she became sick. She was hungry, so she thought, but the food Salvador brought her from the hotel dining room suited her no better than the local fish and beans. The rainy season came, and she felt cold all the time, with a cold that her exercises could not banish. The thing inside her had embedded itself at the root of her pelvis where the dancing started, and it numbed her.

Salvador was no comfort. He had adored this woman whom he'd discovered arching and falling on the beach like a reptile at war with itself, this miracle woman with the ropelike limbs. He was younger than she. Perhaps he thought he'd go among North Americans through her. But he found she was no less vulnerable than the rest: she became poor; she became pregnant; she became sick. He came to her hut one day to find her laughing and crying at the same time. She'd received a letter from her parents. It contained good wishes and news of the children of girls she'd gone to school with. Salvador, not understanding anything but the sweat around her brow which reminded him of his own fear when he went to the army, moved her into the house with his aunt.

There, Anna's money went fast. She was given a bed, while the other woman slept in a hammock and her children on mats. Anna gave money for food. She and Salvador went to movies in town and ate popcorn with pepper sauce. Then he began to leave her at home. He wanted to drink beer with the men now that the baby was showing. So Anna sat in the courtyard behind the house where women much younger than she tended their children. They taught her how to make string bags. There was not one of them who did not have a full womb or an infant suspended down her back in a shawl. She began to fear that she would never get away from the women and back to her man.

Anna was in the final third of her pregnancy when she wrote the second letter. In the now unfamiliar English she could beg; it would humble her friends before it affected her. "I give birth in a few months," she wrote. "If I am to go to the hospital, I must have a lot of money. Please help me. After I have the baby I will come home." She did not intend to do this; Salvador could not emigrate because of his record. But she knew what they wanted.

The answer was a long time coming. Anna was inflated and hard as a blown toad, doing little but sleeping and sitting, when Salvador brought her the reply. This time it was not from Terry but from the business manager of the company. In her clucking private school tone, the woman chided Anna for her irresponsibility and included a small amount of money, as well as a note representing an air ticket for herself only, which she could pick up at Mérida. The administrator noted that it had been with some difficulty the dancers has raised this money, as the company itself was in the usual financial trouble.

At that point, Anna smiled. She knew the money had come to her from a supply as inexhaustible as their guilt. Grown wily, she wrote to the travel agent in Mérida explaining that she was pregnant and could not travel now and asking him to refund her the money, as there had been a misunderstanding with Canada. Miraculously, she got the refund. She had money again. She bought meals in the cafés, for she'd begun to feel full of energy and hungry. She bought a motor scooter for Salvador. The rest she stowed in her bag for the baby. He would arrive any day now.

Today, sitting still in the glare of the sun as it came out on the other side of the cloud, Anna in her red cotton skirt with her shawl tight across her shoulders felt content. The sea came up to her toes gently lapping like a tongue. She was roused from some dream that had overtaken her. She filled her chest with air and knelt in the slightly foaming ruffle of the sea. The water here smelt like no ocean she'd known. At waterfronts of east and west coast cities where the company had toured, the sea had been old and rank, with long hair under its surface, like a woman who'd lived alone forever. But here it was crystalline, transparent, except where the patches of oil spread around the ships that came into the harbour.

She was made of water, new and buoyant. She would

bear the baby, a ship within her. There would be no fear, no falling, nothing could be taken away from her. She would have what she wanted. Perhaps Salvador would love her again and find her beautiful. Perhaps she would go away without him.

Whatever happened, this would be Anna's baby. A baby for Anna whose prairie dancing classmates had turned from their lessons to talk of bedlinen and flatware. A baby for Anna whose parents mated against her aloneness. A baby conceived as much in that aloneness as on the dirt-packed floor of the hut where the brave Mexican could lean on one elbow and brush the ants off her skin without relieving the pressure of his hard, elastic stem inside her.

Leaning forward to stand, she cupped one hand under her belly, lifting it. The baby was pressing down, into her thighs. It would not be long now before she had someone who would love her, always.

Tongues

Tongues

No one had asked Ellen a question for hours, and eavesdropping had become the best revenge. The hostess was either sloshed or seriously trying to seduce a Japanese trade officer. Her voice fluted over the general rumble, telling about the time she went to a topless beach in France and everyone but her was a 32A.

"I wasn't about to take my top off," she said, "but I considered taking off my bottom." The Japanese jerked his head up and down, grinning.

The house was narrow and elaborate. The walls and windows were heavily draped with brocade, the tablecloths tassled. The food had been crabs, duchess potatoes, tarts. Ellen stood by the glass doors which were still open to the garden. The sky was violet around the lanterns, black elsewhere. Azaleas were lurid against the peeling salmon of the brick wall. The ivy had its tendrils in every crack. Overhead in the dark trees, "heat bugs", as she had first called them — cicadas — buzzed like shorting electric circuits.

At Ellen's feet giant leaves reflected in the glass: it was hard to tell whether they were inside trying to get out or outside trying to get in. She was of the same two minds. In the corner, a woman was watching her husband reading the news on television. "*Effrayant! effrayant!*" she screamed. Someone else was lying on the kitchen floor. The hostess ended her tale and began to walk down the centre of the room, holding a plate of sausage rolls, her zipper undone from her cleavage to her waist. She did have enormous breasts.

All around, conversations were about the press and about what diplomats did or did not do. For instance they did not rush from spot to spot while on the job; however, they might jog in the morning. Decorum was key. They did not divulge information to journalists, but they did have parties like this where punch was served from a toilet bowl in the centre of the room.

"Can you believe the Americans have exactly one person in Ottawa who can speak French? And she's only a secretary."

"Do you think Jim looks too old? I should have known he'd go this way when I met his mother. Male baldness pattern comes from the maternal side."

The zipper crept below the hostess's belt. As she came toward the swinging light from the garden, the great white mounds of her breasts seemed about to lift out of their moorings, like dirigibles. She didn't look like a diplomat's wife. There might be a story there, thought Ellen, as the woman bore down on her, with her sausage rolls and alarming gap in her jump suit.

"Which one is your husband, and what does he do?" the hostess asked of Ellen, proferring the tray.

Just then the host himself came around the corner, his shirt coming out of his belt, his bare feet sliding in his loafers. He was a slinking intellectual with no ass, from some little town in New Brunswick. He was envied for his power which was the best kind, the invisible kind; you had to be in the embassy to even know such power existed. Outside the embassy, there was no reason it should exist. He probably came home from the office each day, got drunk on tax-free wine, and buried his face in the white balloons of the wife or wife-equivalent; next morning he felt like a million.

The story. She had just overheard that the hostess was not the wife. The wife had not enjoyed life in Washington; she was back in Montreal. The hostess was a friend.

Holding her punch glass between thumb and forefinger, Ellen let the room go out of focus. She was thinking of another time, when she was in a London club. Over the bar there had been a photograph of fat whores in a line, beside her a man with broken front teeth. She had asked him about his teeth. He had fallen off his stool, he said.

"My dear," he said, "I was so anaesthetized, I never felt a thing."

It had been late afternoon. She had turned the other way to talk to a certain Jay. This Jay had confided that his ex-wife Muriel thought he was a square because he was an alcoholic rather than a drug addict. The bar stool with the slit in it, stuffing bulging, reminded him of Muriel; he raised his eyebrows to imply which aspect of Muriel. Muriel had left him; she was an arrogant cow. With her, he had discovered the definition of middle-aged boredom; you spent all your time talking about why you never did it.

There had been green walls and little pink light bulbs in this club. Asking people how it was they had time to drink past three in the afternoon was forbidden. It was a literary hangout, and one came there, apparently, to get ideas.

"Canadian writers? My God, are there more of you? Do you all ever get together to chat? Where do you do it, at Portage and Main?"

That conversation came to mind because it was the same kind as this evening's: malicious, symbolic. It took place in another country, and besides, one party was drunk and would not be held to account. The other party was silent with terrible recall. Conversation was combat. Difficult questions Ellen had been asked: that day in England, "Do they have sexual intercourse in Canada?" Tonight, when the game had been on television, "Do you like baseball, or do you just submit?" When such an offense was launched, the question became simply in what way would she betray herself? Profess a false enjoyment of baseball or give the company the satisfaction of her submission? "Oh I never submit," she said. "Pass the chips, please."

It is quite possible to be too sensitive to words. After all, it was summer and over ninety degrees. Paying much attention to what people said was foolish. And yet. Once the words were out, there they were, and it was so tempting to speculate.

A sincere man, who did not drink and had carefully parted hair, sought her out in her stance by the door. "Ellen," he said, having asked her name, "Ellen, I am a Christian."

He explained further that his faith was being tried. He had worked as a lobbyist for fellow Christians, had been unjustly fired and was not paid. But he was reluctant to call his lawyers because the Bible (1 Corinthians, 1) stipulated that one Christian may not sue another. On top of that, his wife was in bed with a debilitating female ailment. They had prayed. "The Lord's ways are mysterious," he said.

"We are rejoicing in our grief."

Ellen asked about his church. It was an alliance of congregations: the preachers were known for speaking in tongues. To speak in tongues was an honour, proof of closeness to God. It took the form of a seizure: one shook, vomited, and words came out in an unknown language. Usually one passed out shortly after. As the man moved off, he said to Ellen, "I love you very much."

Ellen pondered the conversation. Very often people are speaking in tongues, but we don't realize they are because the words are ones we know. We believe something obvious to have been said, but that is not at all the case. Of course, when "I love you" does not mean "I love you", it does not necessarily mean "I hate you." Usually there is some oblique, symbolic relationship between the words and the intended message. For instance the utterance, "I love you" may have meant "Thank you for listening" or "I am a better person than you are." Interpreting speech was like trying to understand punch served in a toilet bowl. The presentation is arresting, resonant of this or that, but what, after all, does it say?

A woman came up then and began to tell Ellen about how her husband left her. For ten years of marriage he did not say he was unhappy or that he didn't like her smell or that he would have preferred a blonde. That he was offered a transfer he did not say; that he took it, gave notice on their apartment, cancelled their credit cards, and got himself a place to live in the new city he still didn't say. His work buddies didn't say anything about it either: perhaps they assumed that she knew, perhaps they did not want to meddle. The day came, and he went to Houston. She found out the rest later.

People speak a great deal, some almost constantly.

Often, however, they fail to arrive at their main point. What Ellen wanted to ask was, what did he say during the time he was planning his escape — "Christmas at your folks would be OK.?" Most likely he said, "I love you very much."

Ellen heard the scream even above the noise of the Cajun singer on the record, above the sounds of the host and hostess who were at that point staging a mock rape. Others heard it too. They lowered the volume on the stereo and listened for the siren that should follow the scream. There had been sirens all night long. It was because of proximity to hospitals (and not to crimes and accidents), people said. The house was in a lovely development at the edge of the ghetto, the ghetto being us, people laughed, not them. The rest of the city was out there agitating, incomprehensibly resentful.

The scream came again, turning to repeated sharp screams turning to gurgles. Someone was being mugged, possibly stabbed.

We should call 911, people agreed. They lifted the heavy drapes but could not see out until all the lights inside were turned off. And then there they were, diplomats and press people, peeking around the curtain of a darkened house at an incident in the street. It was unbecoming. At last two men went out the door. Several more stood on the porch. Someone telephoned. They waited. There were more shouts and rustles from down the street. And in minutes, the sound of the siren, as they had expected. There was relief all around; it was indeed a well-patrolled area: important people lived nearby.

The men came back, chagrined. "It was nothing," they said. At first it had appeared that a man was choking a prostitute. He called out that she had stolen his wallet. As the samaritans approached, however, he had pulled a knife on them, and the woman took their wallets, as well as their watches and jewellery. Then the thieves ran away together. The police, when they arrived, confirmed that it was a trick that had been played before.

The party continued. Ellen became involved in a conversation with Jean-Pierre about the language problem. The language problem came up, for him, when he had to speak English. He did not feel like himself. Expressions of emotion were difficult in his second language. He could not offer witty jokes. He could not jam words together and come up with something new, like "stagflation", as those whose native tongue was English could do. Therefore he always felt, while speaking English, as if he were someone else, not Jean-Pierre.

Ellen respected that. She never spoke French, nor indeed Arabic, for the same reasons. She did not like her personality as it struggled through her limitations in other languages. Of course any language poses difficulties. It was just that she had become accustomed to her own shortcomings as they were expressed in her mother tongue. It was essential, as well, that Jean-Pierre feel free. She wanted to say to him, "You must speak in French. I, however, am free to understand only in English."

Ellen told Jean-Pierre about the occasion when she had had to make a little speech and felt it should be in both languages. Before she began the French, however, she was interrupted. An onlooker said, "You did well enough, but I could see how frightened you were because of your tortured hands." Ellen replied that she had been nervous about bursting into French. "Oh, you poor dear," said the onlooker, "is that what happens to you in front of crowds?" As if she had said burst into hives.

When Ellen was young she had believed that in the whole world, only people from Western Canada spoke English without an accent. She had heard this said and had not understood it as a relative statement, as meaning "To me, only people from Western Canada . . ." She had observed, after all, that Torontonians spoke differently, with an accent, as did Englishmen and people from Chicago, while her friends in the west spoke as she did. Jean-Pierre and she agreed that one had only to travel away from where one was born to discover that the accent was their own. Beauty may be in the eye of the beholder, but accent is in the mouth of the offender. Many aspects of language offend. We endure. We persevere with conversation, that's the wonder of it, but in many cases a certain degree of numbness is necessary.

Numbness, alcohol can provide. The party was arriving at its destination, a kind of crash landing at 1:30 A.M. Most people were speaking in tongues. Eavesdropping was no longer necessary. People spoke aloud to whomever could hear.

The big-breasted hostess was telling a story about a party she'd attended where the wife had a new baby. By now she had left her Japanese admirer in the dust; however, several men still encircled her. Late on in the evening, the hostess related, this wife went upstairs, woke up the baby (*Woke Up* the *Baby*!?, was how she said it) and brought him down to nurse. "Then she bared this withered little tit and held it out like a syringe!" she complained.

There was silence. Thoughtful looks came on the faces of the people nearby. Even at that point in the evening, the remark called attention to itself. It begged interpretation: of all that had been hinted at that night, this one perhaps might translate. The hostess seemed to be very angry at the wife for nursing her baby, for having small breasts, for showing them in public. Was she jealous of the baby? Of the status of wife? In either case breasts seemed to be the focus of her rage. Perhaps it was all connected, and the woman was really saying, "How unfair! Here I am with my superior endowments, doomed to be a foreigner, a mistress, while another, scrawnier woman is landed, legitimized and allowed to procreate!" Perhaps her real complaint was underemployment. She may have been in effect telling the men, "Look at my wonderful sexy breasts. Take me to bed, and I will be your wife, your mother." But the voice was so loud and demanding, it seemed that she was calling over the men's heads to other women, perhaps to Ellen herself, conspicuously pregnant. "Pity me! It's your fault; because of women like you I am left outside the doors."

Ellen's husband nearby, giving eye signals: "Are you ready to go home?" She gulped her drink. For Ellen, alcohol was not always enough. Tonight it would not be. Already she could hear the insomnia tape she had from her doctor.

"Close your eyes and listen to my voice," the doctor intoned. "You will notice you feel a certain desire to move . . ." To make his tape sound sleepy, the doctor had recorded his voice and then slowed the speed, which resulted in a low ghoulish tone. Especially elongated were words describing various parts of the body. "Tighten your *caaalf* muscles, your *thiiighs*, your *aaaabdomen*, your *baaaack*, your shoulders. Each time you let go, enjoy the relief."

Between his speeches, caught and made permanent, was the squealing of cars on the pavement in front of his office. After an interlude of traffic, the doctor's voice came back. "When a thought intrudes, simply observe it without particular concern. Become an onlooker to the images and thoughts that are on your mind. Gradually give up the will to do something about these concerns."

Sociology

Sociology

On the porch Ellen stood without looking behind her, like a pack horse at a crossing where she'd stopped many times before. Alec came up the steps: she heard the clinking as his hands sorted the keys from the change in his pocket. Then she heard a low, drawling voice.

"You folks stay right where you are, and this gun ain't going off. You keep right on looking at that door."

She supposed it was time this happened. Their house was in what you called a transition area: you couldn't afford to buy there any more, but you weren't supposed to live there yet. Ellen enjoyed living there, however. She was morbidly fascinated by the differences in circumstances between themselves and the next door neighbour who sat on his steps after dark and raised Newfoundland fishing songs to the sky. It fit with her view of the world, which was that as close as your hand were people who were not as lucky as you and therefore would like to kill you.

The man with the gun came up the stairs. He found Alec's wallet and took it. He took Ellen's purse. He asked for Alec's watch. The watch was gold with a gold band; it had been his father's, awarded for forty year's work in the factory in Quebec. Having died two months after retirement, his father had never worn it. When Alec reached 21 without a cigarette, his mother added the gold band and gave it to her only son. Wordlessly, Alec snapped it off his wrist and handed it over. Ellen groaned. Then the gunman got greedy.

"Your jewellery too," he said. He took a handful of Ellen's hair and pulled it back to see if she was wearing earrings. She wasn't. She had only a couple of rings, her wedding band and one other, which was a pearl she'd gotten for her sixteenth birthday. Earlier that month the pearl had become tight, and she had switched it to a smaller finger. Now she pulled and got it off. The wedding ring was hopeless.

"I can't get it off," she said to the mugger. "My fingers are swollen because I'm pregnant."

She looked him in the eye as she said the word pregnant. She felt she had never been in such danger; she had to enunciate the point of greatest risk. She was testing. It had been her fantasy during these last months that she would run into one of those maniacs who shot pregnant women in the belly or cut them open with a knife.

But the mugger looked back at her with a disinterested rage. Perhaps he would shoot her finger off and get the ring that way. It was still early in the evening, however, and a man was walking by only fifteen feet away, so the mugger just snarled and ran off.

Ellen and Alec attended pre-natal classes in a boys' club

gymnasium in Cabbagetown. Alongside nine other pregnant women Ellen lay on the gym floor on a blanket brought from home and practised breathing patterns to prepare herself for labour. Her head on the pink and blue flowered pillowcase from their bedroom, she raised her hips and lowered them again; the water balloon that was her stomach went up and down. Then she got on hands and knees and Alec rolled tennis balls on her back as she humped it up and down like a dog trying to vomit. The idea was to make the birth natural.

They kept this up for six consecutive Thursdays. On the whole Ellen was disappointed in the classes. It was not the material so much as the other people. She'd thought their common predicament would promote instant friendship, but it had not. This was not for lack of effort on the part of the instructor, Riva, who used the word "share" frequently. By the end they would develop a limited closeness, like that of people stuck together in a train which is liable to go off the tracks. But where they came from, where they would go afterward would not be mentioned.

Ellen tried to pin down some information. She learned that Gloria and Ted were born-agains. She divined that Miriam was at least forty and was not married to the man she came with. She explained them to Alec, who disapproved of her curiosity. The only ones she could not explain were Robert and June.

June was tall with blonde hair and moved hesitantly, but gracefully. Her eyes were cloudy blue. Sometimes the irises darted back and forth as if panicked, but Ellen did not believe she saw anything at all, not even light and shadow, because of the way she held her head. The way she held her head was the best part about her. Her carriage was like that of a large and elegant bird, her head alert and still as if she were listening for an alarm. Her seeing-eye dog lay at her feet, so devoted that he made the husband look like a redundancy. Robert was thickset, pimply, and sullen, and he watched June all the time.

June gave what the rest withheld; she laughed, she talked her fear. Ellen remembered best the day she sat on her metal stacking chair like an oracle, transparent eyelids showing the darting of sightless eyes. "I can't believe it's me who's pregnant," she said. "I suppose because I've never seen myself."

But isn't that what it's like, Ellen thought.

On the last night of class they watched a film of natural childbirth. Someone had brought popcorn, and they stared at the screen, silently passing the bucket. In the dark room Ellen could hear Robert's nasal voice very softly telling June what was being shown. "The baby is coming out of the mother's body," he said. Ellen and Alec both cried. Ellen thought that most of the other people in the class did too. She didn't know for sure though because when the lights went up, she didn't want to look too closely at their faces.

Riva packed the projector, and the women and their supporters made ready to leave. Swollen feet pushed back into bulging shoes; knees poked out to ten and two o'clock as legs strained to lift the immobile trunks. Stomachs first, they walked; the hard, heavy egg shapes pushing flesh away from the centre up to chest, arms, puffing the cheeks. Eyes red from strain, the ten making each other seem more grotesque than ever, the women made ready to go alone into the perilous future.

In the hospital, Ellen forgot all about her childbirth training and began screaming for an anaesthetic. The baby was two weeks late and labour was being induced with a drug. "This baby must like you a lot," said the doctor, turning up the dose again. "He doesn't want to be born." When he came, he wasn't breathing, so the nurse grabbed him and ran down the hall. "My mother always said the cord around the neck meant they're lucky," said Alec. Ellen lay draped in green sheets, being stitched up by the doctor. She felt robbed, raped, aching, and empty. She told Alec it was just like being mugged, and they both began to laugh.

"Tell that to Riva," he said.

"But I don't feel bad. I feel — purified."

"Anyone who feels purified after a mugging has a bad case," said Alec.

In two hours they brought Alain back, cleaned up and swathed in a little white flannel blanket with a toque on his head to keep in the heat. Ellen began to think of the others in the class and how it would be for them. "I wonder what the odds are in ten births," she said, holding her son.

The party was at their place. There had been an RSVP on the invitation, but by the evening before, Ellen had only heard from seven of the ten couples. They were bringing potluck, and she wanted to know how many paper plates to get. She found the class list with the telephone numbers.

The first thing she discovered was that Miriam's phone had been disconnected. Ellen began to feel superstitious. The idea of losing track of one of the group, of not knowing about one of Alain's peers, startled her. She called information and found Miriam's new listing. When she reached it, it turned out she had a new baby boy, and everything was perfectly all right.

Ellen's confidence returned. She decided to call the others she hadn't heard from. The Uruguayan woman had a girl, but Ellen didn't understand any of the details because of the language problem. She hung up and dialed June. The telephone rang seven times, and no one answered.

That was odd; there was always someone home when you have a new baby. She waited until after dinner and then tried again. This time Robert answered. Ellen felt irritated by the sound of his voice; that was when she realized how much she wanted to speak with June. But she said who she was to Robert and asked if they were coming to the party.

Robert cleared a rasp from his throat. Then he sucked in air. "I might as well be straight with you," he said. "We lost our baby."

"Oh my God," said Ellen. "I'm so sorry. I'm so sorry to intrude."

"We got the invitation," he said, continuing as if she hadn't spoken, "and we thought about coming. June wanted to, but I didn't."

Ellen was silent. "But anyway," he said, "it's kind of you to call."

"Oh no, no I shouldn't have. I had no idea."

"June didn't want to tell people. She wanted them just to find out," he said, "naturally." Oh of course it would be natural, thought Ellen, and at whose expense? She was ready to cry with embarrassment. She was dying to know what happened too, but she couldn't ask. "I am very sorry to intrude," she said again, more firmly. "It's a terrible thing."

"Yes," said Robert.

Then no one said anything. Robert started the conversation again with greater energy. "But that doesn't stop me from asking about your baby."

"We had a little boy," Ellen said, "and he's just fine." She didn't tell Robert about the fright they'd had when Alain didn't breathe. It didn't seem proper to have complaints when you had a live son.

"Congratulations," said Robert. "Your baby will bring you a lifetime of happiness." His tone was mean, humble but punishing. Ellen wanted to tell him that their lifetimes would never be so exclusive as he imagined, especially not now, but she didn't.

It was only as she told Alec that Ellen got mad. "Riva knew; she could have spared me that call; why didn't she tell me?"

"Maybe sparing you wasn't her concern," said Alec. He had not been in favour of holding this reunion. The incident only confirmed his belief that coming too close to strangers was asking for trouble. But he was sympathetic. He stood in the kitchen, holding Alain very tightly against his chest, and comforted his wife.

At noon the next day the new parents began to come up the narrow sidewalk. It was funny how nine babies looked like a mob. The oldest was three months, the youngest three weeks. Two of them had great swirls of black hair, but most were bald like Alain. One baby, born by Caesarian to the born-agains, had an angelic, calm face, but most were pinched and worried, unused to life on the outside. All through the house babies bounced on shoulders, slept on laps, sat propped in their infant seats. Now that it was all over, the parents could talk. They told birth stories about the heroism of wives, the callousness of physicians. Those whose babies slept through the night gloated over those whose babies didn't. It turned out one man was a lawyer like Alec and even had an office in the same block. One couple had a live-in already, and about half the women were going back to work.

Ellen got the sociology she wanted all along, and she was happy. Word had gone around about June, and everyone agreed it was better she hadn't come because it would have put such a damper on the party. The story was that she'd been two weeks overdue and had to go in for tests. At her second test the doctor told her the baby was dead. The worst part, all agreed, must have been having to carry the dead baby for another week. Finally June went through a difficult labour. There was nothing wrong with the baby that anyone could see.

When they told the story the women's eyes connected, and their lips pressed down. It was as if a train had crashed and the person in the next seat had been crushed. They could not help but feel relief, lucky to have been missed. But with luck came fear that luck would not last, and the long, hard oval of dread that had quickened in Ellen along with her offspring was born.

Ellen wanted a picture of the babies together. They put Alain out first, in the corner of the couch, propped on his blanket. Others followed with Lila, Andrew, Evelyn, Adam, Ashley, Orin, Jackson, and William, nine prizes all in a row. Their heads bobbed down or dropped to the side; their mouths were open in round O's of astonishment. They fell asleep, leaning on their neighbour or they struck out with spastic hands and hit his face without knowing.

The parents had their cameras ready. They began to shoot pictures, laughing all the while. The line of babies was the funniest thing people had seen in ages. No one had imagined how funny it would be. The babies were startled. They looked not at each other but at the roomful of hysterical adults. One toppled, and the one next to him fell over onto him. Then the whole line began to collapse. Strange creatures with faces like cabbages and changing goblin shapes, tightly rolled in blankets or drooping into puddles of chin and stomach, they could have come from an alien star. The parents laughed, with relief at their babies' safe landing, and wonder at who they might be. The flashbulbs kept popping as the nine silly little bodies toppled and began to run together into a heap, until one of them, Evelyn, Ellen thinks it was, began to cry.

Palm Beach

Palm Beach

An east wind today. The beach is dotted with lacy blue ears. Walter calls them sailors. They are acid and will sting, like the man of war. But they are only dangerous for a little while; they are dying, like everything washed up here, says Walter. He gesticulates further in the wind and walks away. Walter does the beach.

Voices here all lose themselves in surf, messages half completed. But what surf! The vicious curl of the waves, the undertow, the frothy roll onto sand so fresh it could have come yesterday. Down near the edge the sand is firm to the foot; it shifts only after the water has drained through. The slick reflects a grey sky; further out the water towers like some oil painting, Storm at Sea.

Head down, Sheila returns from her walk to the cabana where the children huddle with their nanny. An imported girl, she has hung her Union Jack T-shirt on a lounge chair as advertisement. Her posture — knuckles buried in sand, chin down — speaks unhappiness. No compatriot has appeared.

"Is 'er a prize for the best sandcastle on the beach?" the girl wants to know. "A week for one in Bermuda?"

"You're in Palm Beach, there's no better place."

Winn jerks her head in disbelief.

Unpleasant girl, thinks Sheila. *It was a mistake to bring her. From some little town in Yorkshire, she'd never see this in a million years if we didn't. It's a plummy job.*

Sheila remonstrates with the harsh inner voice. Perhaps Winn's unhappiness is not exactly about the job. It's about — what — fortune. Something struck her as soon as they walked into the condominium. It had to do with the palms, the bay windows over the sand. When she saw the elevator, she suppressed a whoop, and then her face closed. Why should she work when others were on holiday? Right now, she would like to find a pub, meet a boy, and join the club. She says it all in the incline of her head. "What is this club of fortunates, and why can I not be in it?"

Mac strolls up, still tall with feet lost in sand. He speaks aside, but his voice is the only one which carries. "Get her off the beach," he says. "She's going to fry herself and tomorrow she'll be useless."

"You can't hire out the care of your children," says Sheila. "You end up with another one to think about is all."

Mac raises his hands, chiding. "Thinking! If breathing were all you had to do, then you'd worry about breathing. This is supposed to be a rest for you. Enjoy. The wind will drop tonight."

In the end it is more than thinking. Someone has to keep it all in mind. And that becomes occupation, an occupation by forces.

Inside, the sudden sun falls in squares on yellow rug and beach pail, on red, green, blue, the bright primaries of building blocks. The little boy can stack five now to make a tower, then balance his bottle on top. See! He smiles brilliantly, showing his mother.

"Come here," says Sheila, "you are beautiful and so clever."

He gives his mother a kiss, light as breath, and solemn.

Not yet two, and you feel my sadness. I must be careful.

The infant tugs at her breast. They communicate this way — the baby fierce, insisting; the woman stopped, dull as a cow. Later the baby cries, and they come together once more. "Hello again, tendril arms and jerky, pushing feet," says Sheila. "Hello new, crumpled thing. There now, swallow me." The mouth closes on her nipple. "This is motherhood, you too may have it."

"You shouldn't talk to her that way," says Mac, pretending to watch T.V.. "You shouldn't be sarcastic with children."

"She likes to hear me. It calms her."

Peeking under his drooping eyelids, Mac can see his wife's face, her tight, tired mouth. He would go to her, put his arms around her, lift her to his chest, but these days she hates it when he touches her. The babies take so much. Poor Sheila. If he had breasts, he would do some of the feeding. He wonders how Sheila knows the baby likes to hear her voice.

"Lucky you, to be so sure," he says.

Sheila shuts her eyes. The inner voice, softer now, takes her to that day two months ago when she first saw her baby.

You, never so much my own as in the moment you left me. We were locked. Out, out, I groaned, forcing, such power. But delicately, secretly, I hooked your head with my pelvic bones. Your first double message. Your skull rocked, rocked back and forth in that too narrow cradle, you were battered within me.

The doctor, your father stood by. And this embrace of ours stopped being love, became an emergency. They called at me over some wall. Please push. People rushed about, over there from me. Will the baby make it? Can she push more? Try, woman, try to get the baby down. Hands waited to catch you. I was like the star of some team.

The baby loosens her hold on the nipple, then catches it again. The voice waits and then goes on. *From my mouth came mighty roars. Pushing, pushing. Each inch was cheered. Only I knew about the treacherous holding back, the hooking which had you ear to ear and would not let you turn, dive for air. Just these few more minutes together, baby. They were all bystanders then, who before had owned you with their imaginings and later would claim you for their world. Then it was our show and I couldn't let you go, you who had no sex to me but were only the hard bunt of life in throes.*

The baby's mouth pops off the nipple. Her head falls back, sated. Sheila doesn't move. *That much I remember. But how did it all end? They had to stop us somehow, go in with their machinery and get you. Then the ejaculation — a cliché, but not to be avoided. "It's a girl!" We rejoiced while, clenched up tight like a purple fist, you cried. Then against my breast you suddenly went soft, and I thought — Girl.*

Sheila sits up, wiping her eyes. She has been asleep with the baby. The boy crawls to her, driving a truck to her foot, then up her ankle. She asks him to leave her, to play with his blocks, see his daddy, anything, but not to bump the baby. He pushes the truck up her leg. Vroom, vroom. Where does it come from, this universal boy's game? Who taught him to say that? The baby wails. Mac scolds the boy. Now Sheila, the boy, and the baby are crying.

"Oh, God," says Mac. "Let me out of here."

Winn, folding sheets in the corner, has a small smile on

her face. Controlling her tears, Sheila looks at her, hard. She wants me to suffer parenthood properly, she thinks. She doesn't want my lot to be eased at all, not by her or by anything. How did she get to be so mean, so young?

But now it is five o'clock and Winn is off duty. She goes to her room, turns on the radio loud, and leaves the door open. The boy wanders there. Sheila sees him; but does not stop him. Off duty is off duty, however, and he is rebuffed. Curious, arms swinging, he returns to Sheila. "Mama."

Minutes later, Winn appears, spraying herself with perfume. She want to chat, she wants advice. In the bars, she says, British nannies have a reputation for being fast. First question, what do you do? Second question, do you live in? "If you live in, they ger' on to someone else because you can't bring men home."

Sheila and Mac look at each other. What is she asking? Do I have to deal with this too? Sheila signals. Mac waves his hand.

"You may not," Sheila says, "not here, not now." And the girl retreats.

But is that fair, she asks herself? Here you are, a married woman, settled, with all of this and two fragrant babies winding over me on the cushions. Winn has nothing. "Winn needs something of her own," she says, hearing the door shut. "A man . . ."

"She won't find one," says Mac. "Not with her attitude. She comes on as such a loser. The stories she tells! The wrong visa, lost key, bounced cheque, the missed call." He is folding the laundry which Winn left half finished. "Look, that Union Jack T-shirt ran blue all over our tennis stuff. She didn't even apologize. Just grinned and said something about her luck."

Then suddenly, Winn is gone. The babies too, first one to bed and then the other. Mac gets a headache. He thinks it might be sunstroke, the rays can get to you, even through a cloud cover. He goes to bed. There is no one left but Sheila. Night is falling. The house is silent, a glassy cockpit jutting over the sea which eats away at the foot of the dunes. She paces, hugging herself. A shadow crosses the carpet; it is the security guard who prowls the path above the sea. She pulls the curtain. Now she is closed in. She paces some more and then slides open the door.The sea booms. She breaks out.

Ecstatic, guilty, down the beach she walks. The wind parts her hair from the nape forward. She walks to a place between the larger houses, infrequently visited by their owners, and finds a bit of scruff on the dune. She sits. The sand is warmer than the air. It curves ahead of her to the towers of Boynton Beach.

There would be people there. Here, she was too much attended or too much alone. Behind her, privacy is maintained by guard dogs as tall as horses which howl over the walls of empty mansions. In front, an ocean full of stinging ears stretches all the way to Europe, Africa. The sand leaves a narrow margin for lovers, narrower yet when lovers breed babies, nannies, washing machines, and sunburn. It is no longer possible to meet the sunrise a simple two, as they did the first time. It was dark, they dug themselves down in the sand, and the waves crept up like a coverlet. After, he shaved his moustache so she could see his lip. It was thinner than the bottom one, but turned up impishly in the corners. She was in love. They promised all this, to love, work, have children together.

She had no secret to bare for him, or so it seemed. A simple thirty-year-old, tired of freedom. A small unobtrusive career, a bendable sort of life. *Hah! Now we know different.* She is the mystery, she is the magician, producing tokens from private places. Babies from her crotch, like dazzling baubles from ear or mouth, unbreakable in the palm. Words, scratched in haste, taken for grocery lists. Words to be polished, kept, sent to strangers. Words they both fear; they refuse to lie.

She stands up and starts to walk. The sea-noise is less; the voice, which had been an irritation, is beginning to be comforting. Could it be my old unhappiness speaking? she wonders. At that moment she rather misses it. It had a texture, it had nerve ends, it had motivation. Why not be a lonely working woman again? Be like Winn, on the outside, with evenings free, instead of being — like this — all tied up in the centre with a deadly need to write. She read *Jane Eyre.* It is rather awkward, all that governess literature, and her on the wrong side of the equation.

This thought pleases her, its ironic possibilities. She turns back. Climbs the beach stairs to the paved paths, nods to the guard as she threads her way among the lighted discs at knee-height. She passes the open door. Tours the actual kidney-shaped pool, passes the door again. Goes to the end of the path and tells herself to go in. It is late, and she is tired, but she cannot stop.

At last she switches on the fluorescent light in front of the mirror. There springs a disappointed face, green eyes slightly reddened with wine or sun, tight brow, downpressed mouth. It is not me, Sheila insists. It will not be me. She switches off the light and stands, her form silver and cold in the glass. This is my only life. I must go on. Go to bed.

He is awake.

A perfect day this time. Sunlight streams like banners from the windows; they read the *Palm Beach Times* and drink coffee. Mrs. Somebody Someone took her two sable coats out of storage thinking to sell one. I don't really need two, she says, but they're too beautiful to give up. And put them back. Mac and Sheila laugh, united now by the night, the few hours when there was no one but them. Winn, her hands in the sink, views it all as the strange rituals of foreign folk and does not mind. She met a fellow working in the Pro Shop; he is from Manchester.

The boy is building towers again, six and seven blocks high. He knocks them down and laughs. Mac helps him put them up.

The ocean too is patient today. They all go to the beach. The sailors are gone; Walter has raked the debris from the storm into piles and is pushing it back into the tide. Although there is a yellow flag up, for man of war, they try the water.

''It's hard to ger' in,'' says Winn, ''but when you ger' in you don't want to ger' out.''

Chesty pelicans glide, dive but not dive, collapse as if shot, beak first into the shallows. The little boy points. Up in the sky a twin engine draws a tail: ''See Our Bikinis at Parrot Eyes.'' And higher still in the palmy air five jets in formation spell ''We are the Miller Squardron.'' Skywriting gets the message across.

Someone runs down the beach shouting. ''Shark in the water, get out!'' Winn takes the children up to the cabana. Mac and Sheila believe he cries wolf and go in anyway. At the place where the waves begin to crest, she turns her back on them.

''Here comes one!''

And the huge blue-white wall breaks over her like a load

of fine china. She goes down, she is tumbled, taken in and then rejected, spat forward, a projectile. She scrabbles for the bottom and finds it. She gains her feet as the world slips backward under her and comes out on top. She always comes out on top.

PENGUIN · SHORT · FICTION

OTHER TITLES IN THIS SERIES

The Day is Dark/Three Travellers
Marie-Claire Blais

Cafe le Dog
Matt Cohen

High Spirits
Robertson Davies

The Pool In the Desert
Sara Jeannette Duncan

Dinner Along the Amazon
Timothy Findley

Penguin Book of Canadian Short Stories
edited by Wayne Grady

Treasure Island
Jean Howarth

Moccasin Telegraph
W.P. Kinsella

The Thrill of the Grass
W.P. Kinsella

Champagne Barn
Norman Levine

Melancholy Elephants
Spider Robinson